Ivy took the glass of champagne he was holding for her. "It's Friday night," she reminded him. "Wouldn't all the restaurants that serve superb meals be fully booked?"

"There's not a maître d' in Sydney who wouldn't find a table for me," he answered, with supreme arrogance.

She sipped the champagne, and the fizz went to her head, promoting the urge to be reckless. "All right," she said slowly. "I will have dinner with you."

A treacherous tingle of anticipation invaded Ivy's entire body. She didn't wait to hear him make arrangements, pretending it was irrelevant to her whether or not he secured a table for the promised dinner. Undoubtedly he would. Jordan Powell could probably buy his way into anything, anytime at all.

But he couldn't buy her.

## All about the author...
### *Emma Darcy*

**EMMA DARCY**'s life journey has taken as many twists and turns as those of the characters in her stories, whose popularity worldwide has resulted in sixty million books in print.

Born in Australia, and currently living on a beautiful country property in New South Wales, she has moved from country to city to towns and back to country, sporadically indulging her love of tropical islands with numerous vacations.

Her ambition to be an actress was partly satisfied when she played in amateur theater productions, but ultimately fulfilled when she became a writer. Now she has the exciting pleasure of playing all the roles, as well as directing them and ringing down the curtain calls.

Initially a teacher of French and English, she changed her career to computer programming before marriage and motherhood settled her into community life. Her creative urges were channeled into oil painting, pottery, and designing and overseeing the construction and decorating of two homes, all in the midst of keeping up with three lively sons and the very busy social life of her businessman husband.

A voracious reader, the step to writing her own books seemed a natural progression to Emma, and the challenge of creating wonderful stories was soon highly addictive. With her strong interest in people and relationships, Emma found the world of romance fiction a happy one.

Currently she has broadened her horizons and begun to write mainstream women's fiction. Other new directions include her most recent adventures of blissfully breezing around the Gulf of Mexico from Florida to Louisiana in a red convertible, and risking the perils of the tortuous road along the magnificent Amalfi Coast in Italy.

# *Wife in Public*

## EMMA DARCY

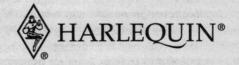

# HARLEQUIN®

TORONTO • NEW YORK • LONDON
AMSTERDAM • PARIS • SYDNEY • HAMBURG
STOCKHOLM • ATHENS • TOKYO • MILAN • MADRID
PRAGUE • WARSAW • BUDAPEST • AUCKLAND

Recycling programs
for this product may
not exist in your area.

ISBN-13: 978-0-373-12977-5

WIFE IN PUBLIC

Previously published in the U.K. as HIDDEN MISTRESS, PUBLIC WIFE

First North American Publication 2011

Copyright © 2010 by Emma Darcy

This edition published by arrangement with Harlequin Books S.A.

For questions and comments about the quality of this book
please contact us at Customer_eCare@Harlequin.ca.

® and TM are trademarks of the publisher. Trademarks indicated with
® are registered in the United States Patent and Trademark Office, the
Canadian Trade Marks Office and in other countries.

www.eHarlequin.com

Printed in U.S.A.

# WIFE IN PUBLIC

# CHAPTER ONE

'THE Valentino king of rose-giving is on the loose again,' Heather Gale remarked, swinging around from her computer chair to grin at Ivy. 'He's just ordered the sticky date and ginger fudge with the three dozen red roses to go to his current woman. That's his goodbye signature. Take it from me. She's just been crossed out of his little black book.'

Ivy Thornton rolled her eyes over her sales manager's salacious interest in Jordan Powell's playboy activities. Ivy had met him once, very briefly at her mother's last gallery exhibition of her paintings. That had been two years ago, soon after her father had died and she'd been coming to grips with running the rose farm without his guidance.

Much to her mother's disgust, she'd worn jeans to the showing, completely disinterested in competing with the socialites who attended such events. For some perverse reason Jordan Powell had asked to be introduced to her, which had displeased her mother, having to own up to a daughter who had made no effort to look stunningly presentable.

There'd been curious interest in his eyes, probably because she didn't fit in with the fashionable crowd. The encounter was very minimal. The gorgeous model hugging his arm quickly drew him away, jealous of his attention being directed even momentarily to any other woman.

Understandably.

Keeping him to herself would have been a top-priority aim.

The man was not only a billionaire but oozed sex appeal—twinkling, bedroom blue eyes, perfect male physique in the tall-dark-and-handsome mould, charming voice and manner with a strikingly sensual mouth that had worn a teasing quirk of amusement as he'd spoken to Ivy. No doubt, with his wealth and looks, the world and everyone in it existed for his amusement.

'How long did this love interest last?' she asked, knowing Heather enjoyed keeping tabs on his affairs. Jordan Powell was the rose farm's biggest spender on the private-client list.

Heather turned eagerly back to the computer to check the records. 'Let's see…a month ago he ordered jelly beans with the roses so that meant he wanted her to lighten up and just have fun. She probably didn't get the message, hence the parting of the ways. A month before that it was the rum and raisin fudge, which indicates the heavy-sex stage.'

'You can't really know that, Heather,' Ivy dryly protested.

'Stands to reason. He always starts off with the double chocolate fudge when he first sends roses to a new woman. Clearly into seduction at that point.'

'I don't think he needs to seduce anyone,' Ivy muttered, thinking most women would willingly fall at his feet, given one ounce of encouragement.

Heather was not to be moved from her deductions. 'Probably not, but I think some play hard to get for a little while,' she explained. 'Which is when he sends the roses with the macadamia fudge, meaning she's driving him nuts so please come to the party. This last one didn't get the macadamia gift.'

'Therefore an easy conquest,' Ivy concluded.

'Straight into it I'd say,' Heather agreed. 'And that was…almost three months ago. He didn't stick with her very long.'

'Has he ever stuck with any woman very long?'

'According to my records, six months has been the top limit so far, and that was only once. The usual is two to four months.'

She twirled the chair back to face Ivy, who was seated at her office desk, trying to get her mind into work mode but hopelessly distracted by the conversation which touched on sore points from her mother's most recent telephone call. Another gallery exhibition. Another shot of advice to sell the rose farm and get a life in Sydney amongst interesting people. Insistence on a shopping trip so she could feel proud of her daughter's appearance.

The problem was she and her mother occupied different worlds, had done so for as long as Ivy could remember. Her parents had never divorced but had lived separate lives, with Ivy being brought up by her father on the farm, while her mother indulged her need for cultural activities in the city. Horticulture was of no interest to her and she was constantly urging Ivy to leave it behind and experience the full art of living, which seemed to be endless parties with endless empty chatter.

Ivy loved the farm. It was what she knew, what she was comfortable with. And she had loved her father, loved him sharing the farm with her, teaching her everything about it. It was a good life, giving a sense of satisfaction and achievement. The only thing missing from it was a man she could love, and more importantly, one who loved her back. She had thought, believed... but no, Ben hadn't supported her when she'd needed support.

'Hey, maybe you'll get to meet our rose Valentino again at your mother's exhibition! And he'll be free this time!' Heather said with a waggish play of her eyebrows.

'I very much doubt a man like him would turn up on his own,' Ivy shot back at her, instantly pouring cold water over ridiculous speculation.

It didn't dampen Heather's cheerful outlook on possibilities. 'You never know. I bet you could turn his head if you hung out your hair and dolled yourself up. How often do your see that glorious shade of red-gold hair? If you didn't wear it in a plait, the sheer mass of it would catch his eye.'

'So what if it did?' Ivy loaded her voice with scepticism. 'Do you think for one moment Jordan Powell would be interested in a country farm girl? Or for that matter, I'd be interested in being the next woman on his Valentino list?'

Undeterred, Heather cocked her head on one side consideringly, her hazel eyes sparkling with mischief in the making. Her brown hair was cut in an asymmetrical bob and she tucked the longer side of it behind her ear as she invariably did before getting down to business. She was brilliant at her job, a warm friendly person by nature, and although she was two years older than Ivy—almost at the thirty mark, which was when she planned to have a baby—they'd become close friends since Heather had married Barry Gale, who was in charge of the greenhouses.

She had wanted to work at the rose farm, too, and with her computer skills was a great asset to the business. Ivy thanked her lucky stars that Heather seemed to have dropped out of the heavens when someone to help manage the office work was most needed. It had been a very stressful time after her father had been diagnosed with inoperable cancer. Even knowing his illness was terminal she had not been prepared for his death. The grief, the sudden huge hole in her life…without Heather, she might not have been able to keep everything flowing to maintain the company's reliable reputation.

'Seems to me Jordan Powell could well be up for a new experience and it could be good for you, too, Ivy,' she drawled now, having fun with being provocative.

Ivy laughed. '*Up* is undoubtedly the operative word for him. Even if I did catch his eye, I don't think I'd like the downer that inevitably follows the up. I know his track record, remember?'

'Exactly! Forewarned, forearmed. He won't break your heart since you're well aware he'll move on. You haven't had a vacation for three years, nor had a relationship with a man for over two. Here you are, wasting your prime in work, and if you vegetate too long, you'll forget how to kick up your heels. I bet Jordan Powell could give you a marvellous time—great fun, great sex, an absolutely lovely trip to wallow in for a while. Definitely worth having, if only to give you a different perspective on life.'

'Pie in the sky, Heather. I can't see Jordan Powell making a beeline for me, even if he does turn up alone at the gallery.' She shrugged. 'As for the rest, I have been thinking of taking a trip somewhere now that everything on the farm is running smoothly. I was looking through the travel section of the Sunday newspaper yesterday and...'

'That's it!' Heather cried triumphantly, leaping to her feet. 'Have you still got yesterday's newspapers?'

'In the paper bin.'

'I saw just the thing for you. Wait! I'll find it.'

A few minutes later she was slapping the *Life* magazine from the Sunday *Sun-Herald* down on Ivy's desk. It was already opened at a fashion page emblazoned with the words— *The* it *factor*.

'I was talking about a taking a vacation, not clothes,' Ivy reminded her.

Heather tapped her finger on a picture featuring a model wearing a black sequinned jacket with a wide leather belt cinching in her waist, a pink sequinned mini-skirt, and high-heeled black platform shoes with pink and yellow and green bits attached to straps that ended up around her ankles. 'If you wore this to your mother's exhibition, you'd knock everyone's eyes out.'

'Oh, sure! That pink skirt with my carrot hair? You're nuts, Heather.'

'No, I'm not. The retailer will have other colours. You could buy green instead of pink. That would go with your eyes and still match in with the shoes. It would be brilliant on you, Ivy. You're tall enough and slim enough to carry it off.' She pointed again. 'And look at these long jet earrings. They'd be fabulous swinging in front of your hair which you'll have to wear down like the model. Yours will look a lot more striking against the jacket. The black handbag with the studs is a must, as well.'

'Probably costs a fortune,' Ivy muttered, tempted by the image of herself in such a *wow* outfit, but unable to see herself wearing it anywhere else in the future.

Such clothes simply weren't worn around here. The farm was a hundred kilometres south of Sydney, situated in a valley which had once been a pastoral estate but had become a settlement for hobby farms. Very casual dress was the norm at any social occasion.

'You can afford it,' Heather insisted. 'The farm raked in heaps with the St Valentine's Day sales. Even if it's only a one-off occasion for this gear, why not? Didn't you say your mother wanted you to appear more fashionable at her exhibition this time?'

Ivy grimaced at the reminder. 'So I'd fit in, not stand out.'

Heather grinned. 'Well, I say, sock it to her. And sock it to Jordan Powell if he turns up, too.'

Ivy laughed. On both counts it was terribly tempting.

Sacha Thornton's jaw would probably drop at seeing her daughter look like a trendy siren. It might even silence the barrage of critical advice that Ivy was usually subjected to every time she was with her mother.

As for Jordan Powell—well, there was certainly no guarantee that he'd be there, but…it would be fun to see if she could attract the sexiest man in Australia. It would do her female ego good, if nothing else.

'Okay! Get on your computer and find out from the listed retailers where I can buy all this stuff,' she tossed at Heather, feeling a bubbly sense of throwing her cap over a windmill. And why not? Just for once! She *could* afford it.

'Yes!' Heather punched the air with her fist, grabbed the magazine and danced back to her chair, singing an old Abba tune—'Take a chance on me…'

Ivy couldn't help smiling. If she was going to be mad enough to wear that outfit, she needed to acquire it as fast as possible so she had enough time to practise walking in those crazy shoes. The exhibition opening was this Friday evening, cocktails at six in the gallery. She only had four and a half days to get ready for it.

# CHAPTER TWO

JORDAN Powell sat at the breakfast table, perusing the property sales reported in the morning newspaper as he waited for Margaret to serve him the perfect crispy bacon with the perfect eggs hollandaise that not even the best restaurants had ever equalled. Not to his taste, anyway. Margaret Partridge was a jewel—a meticulous housekeeper and a great cook. He enjoyed her blunt honesty, too. It was a rarity in his life and he wasn't about to lose it. All in all, Margaret was far more worth keeping than Corinne Alder.

The delicious scent of freshly cooked bacon had him looking up and smiling at Margaret as she entered the sunroom where he always ate breakfast and lunch when he was home. There was no smile back. The expression on her face disdained any pleasantries between them this morning. Jordan quickly folded his newspaper and set it aside, aware that Margaret's feathers were seriously ruffled.

She dumped the plate of bacon and eggs in front of him, planted her hands on her hips and brusquely warned, 'If you invite that Corinne Alder back to this house, Jordan, I'm out of here. I will not be talked down to by a good-for-nothing chit like that, thinking she's got it over me just because she was born with enough good looks for you to want her in your bed.'

Jordan raised an open palm for peace. 'The deed is done, Margaret. I finished with Corinne this morning. And I apologise profusely for her behaviour towards you. I can only say in my defence she was as sweet as pie to me and...'

'Well, she would be, wouldn't she?' Margaret cut in with a sniff of disgust at his obvious gullibility. 'I don't mind you having a string of affairs. At least that's more honest than marrying and cheating. You can parade as many women as you like through this house, but I won't be treated with disrespect.'

'I shall make that very clear to anyone I invite in future,' Jordan solemnly promised. 'I'm sorry my judgement of character was somewhat blurred in this instance.'

Margaret sniffed again. 'You could try practising looking beyond the surface.'

'I shall attempt to plumb the depths next time.'

'Out of bed as well as in it,' she whipped back at him.

He heaved a sigh. 'Now is that nice, Margaret? Am I ever anything but nice to you? Haven't I just shown how much I care about your feelings by breaking it off with Corinne?'

'Good riddance!' she declared with satisfaction. 'And it's on account of the fact that you're always nice to me that I didn't burn your breakfast.' A smile was finally bestowed on him. 'Enjoy it!'

On her way out of the sunroom a triumphant mutter floated back to him. 'She had a big bum anyhow.'

Clearly a flaw to true physical beauty in Margaret's mind. It left Jordan's mouth twitching with amusement.

Margaret was virtually bumless, a short, skinny woman
in her fifties, totally disinterested in enhancing her femininity. She never wore make-up, was hardly ever out of
the white shirtmaker dresses which she considered a
suitable uniform for her position, along with flat white
lace-up shoes. Her unashamedly grey hair was invariably screwed up into a neat bun on top of her head.
However, she did exude quite extraordinary energy and
there was a lot of sharp intelligence in her bright, brown
eyes, along with the sharp wit that occasionally flew off
her tongue.

Jordan had liked her immediately.

When he had interviewed her for the job she had told
him she was divorced, didn't intend ever to marry again,
and if she had to keep a house and cook for a man, she'd
rather be paid for it. Her two children were doing fine
for themselves and she liked the idea of doing fine for
herself, being employed by a billionaire in a house full
of luxuries. If he would give her a month's trial, she
would prove he'd be lucky to find anyone better.

Jordan considered himself very lucky to have found
Margaret. He especially appreciated how fortunate he
was as he tucked into his superbly cooked breakfast.
There were always beautiful women vying for his attention and he enjoyed having a taste of them, but none
of them stayed as constantly delectable as Margaret's
meals.

Corinne could be easily replaced. As for looking for
more than a bed partner…no, he wasn't going down
that road again, having almost been drawn into proposing marriage by the extremely artful Biancha who
had presented herself as the perfect wife for him, so
perfectly obliging to his every need and desire it had
struck a slightly uneasy chord in him, though not enough

to pull him back from the brink until the deception un-
ravelled.

She'd known all along that her father's supposed
wealth was a house of cards about to fall…totally dis-
honest about her family situation…and when the col-
lapse could no longer be held off, it had become sick-
eningly obvious that she had targeted him to be her
rescue package. No way would she have put herself out
so much for the man…without the billions to keep her
life sweet.

Margaret might have spotted Biancha's true colours
if she'd been working for him then. Not much got past
his shrewd housekeeper. In fact, having such a jewel
running his house, he saw no reason whatsoever to
take a wife, especially when he was never short of bed
partners.

Too few marriages worked for long, especially in his
social set, and there was nothing more sour than the
financial fallout that came with divorce. He'd witnessed
enough of those problems with his sister's marriages.
Three times now Olivia had blindly hooked up with
fortune-hunters, not even learning from experience,
which annoyed the hell out of him. As the old saying
went, once bitten should have made her twice shy. A
million times shy in his book!

At least his parents had had the sense to keep their
marriage together, although that had been a different
generation. His father had been very discreet about his
string of mistresses, allowing his mother to maintain
her pride in being the wife of one of the most prominent
property tycoons in Australia and enjoy the pleasure of
the brilliant lifestyle he provided. Besides, she had had
her 'walkers' whenever his father hadn't been available
to accompany her to the opera or the theatre—gay men

who loved the arts as much as she did, and who were delighted to have the privilege of escorting her, thereby getting free tickets.

His parents had kept the bond going for thirty years, and there'd still been some affection between them at the end, his mother genuinely grieving over his father's death. It was a lot of shared years, regardless of the ups and downs. Jordan doubted there was a woman alive who could interest him enough to want to share more than even a few months with her. They invariably turned out to be too damned full of themselves.

I want…I need…look at me…talk to me. If I'm not the centre of your universe, I'm going to sulk or throw a tantrum.

He'd just finished breakfast when his mobile rang. He took it out of his shirt pocket, hoping it wasn't Corinne calling to appeal for some reconsideration. That would be extremely tedious. She'd been nastily dismissive of Margaret's feelings, and he wasn't about to accept any excuse for her rudeness to a highly valued employee.

It was a relief to find it was his mother wanting contact with him.

'Good morning,' he said cheerfully. 'What can I do for you?'

'You can be free this Friday evening to escort me to an art gallery,' she replied with her usual queenly aplomb. It was amazing how many people bowed to her will when she employed that tone. Of course, the wealth backing it had a big influence. Nonie Powell was known to be enormously charitable, and she was not above using that as a power tool.

Jordan, however, did not have to be a courtier. 'What's wrong with Murray?' he demanded, wondering if the 'walker' she most relied upon had somehow lost her favour.

'The poor boy slipped on wet tiles and broke his ankle.'

The poor boy was a very dapper sixty year old.

'I'm sorry to hear that. What's on at what gallery?'

'It's dear Henry's gallery at Paddington. He's showing Sacha Thornton's latest work. You bought two of her paintings at her last exhibition so you should be interested in seeing what she's done more recently.'

He remembered. Lots of vivid colour. A field of poppies in Italy and a vase of marigolds. The paintings had brightened up the walls at the sales office for one of his retirement villages. He also remembered the vivid red-gold hair of Sacha Thornton's daughter. She'd worn jeans. Margaret would have approved of *her* bum. Very neat. But it was the hair that had drawn him into asking for an introduction.

Wrong time, wrong place, with Melanie Tindell hanging on his arm, but Jordan felt a strong spark of interest in meeting the artist's daughter again. Wonderful pale skin—amazingly without freckles—and eyes so green he wouldn't mind plumbing *their* depths. She could have looked spectacular with a bit of effort. He'd wondered why she hadn't bothered. Most women would have played up such natural assets.

The name came back to him...Ivy.

Poison Ivy?

There'd definitely been some tension between her and her mother.

All very curious.

'The doors open at six o'clock,' his own mother informed him. 'Henry will serve us decent champagne and there'll be the usual hors d'oeuvres. If you'll be at home at five-thirty I'll direct my chauffeur to pick you up along the way.'

His current domain at Balmoral was only a slight diversion on his mother's route from Palm Beach. 'Fine!' he replied, deciding he could improvise with alternative transport should Ivy prove interesting enough to pursue.

'Thank you, Jordan.'

'My pleasure.'

He smiled as he closed his mobile and tucked it back in his pocket.

He didn't mind pleasing his mother, especially when there was the possibility of pleasure for himself.

# CHAPTER THREE

Ivy was late. The Friday-evening peak-hour traffic had been horrific, and finding a parking place had been equally frustrating. She had to walk three blocks virtually on her toes in the trendy shoes, silently cursing the designers who dictated foot fashion. They deserved a seat in hell. No, not a seat. They should have to walk forever in their own torturous creations.

As she turned the last corner to the street where the gallery was situated, she saw a chauffeur popping back into a Rolls-Royce which was double-parked outside her destination. *Easy for some,* she thought, her mind instantly zinging to Jordan Powell. Everything would be easy for a billionaire, especially women. Certainly in his case. A fact she was unlikely to forget.

In Heather's lingo, she was a red-hot tamale to-night.

If Jordan Powell was here by himself...if he bit... what should she do?

Have a taste of him or run?

*Wait and see,* she told himself. There was no point in crossing bridges until she came to them.

She switched her thoughts to her mother. It was a big night for her. At least this outfit should not take any of the shine off it. It was sequin city all the way.

Henry Boyce, the gallery owner, was obsequiously chatting up one of his super-wealthy clients when Ivy walked in, but his eagle eye was open for newcomers. When he caught sight of her, his jaw dropped. The gorgeously gowned woman with the perfectly styled blond hair who had lost his attention turned to see who was the distraction, a miffed look on her arrogant face. The man who stood on the other side of her shifted enough to view the intrusive object.

It was Jordan Powell.

And *his* face broke into a delighted grin.

Ivy's heart instantly leapt into a jig that would have rivalled the fastest dance performers in Ireland.

'Good heavens! Ivy?' Henry uttered incredulously, his usual aplomb momentarily deserting him.

'Who?' the woman demanded.

She was considerably older than Jordan, Ivy realised, though beautifully preserved and very full of her own importance.

'Forgive me, Nonie,' Henry rattled out. 'I wasn't expecting…it's Sacha's daughter, Ivy Thornton. Come on in, Ivy. Your mother will be so pleased to see you.'

Not looking like a farm girl this time.

He didn't say it but he was thinking it.

He'd wanted to turn her away from the last exhibition until she'd identified herself.

Ivy recovered enough from the thumping impact of Jordan Powell's presence to smile. 'I'll go through and find her.'

'A pleasure to see you here again, Ivy,' the rose Valentino said, stunning her anew that he actually remembered meeting her before. 'I don't think you met my mother last time,' he continued, stepping around the woman and holding out a beckoning hand to invite

Ivy into the little group. 'Let me introduce you. Nonie Powell.'

His mother. Who looked her up and down as though measuring whether she was worth knowing. She had blue eyes, too, but they had a touch of frost in them, probably caused by the sheer number of women who streamed through her playboy son's life, none of whom stayed long enough to merit her attention.

Ivy's smile tilted ironically as she stepped forward and offered her hand. 'A pleasure to meet you, Mrs Powell.'

'Are you an artist, too, my dear?' she asked, deigning to acknowledge Ivy with a brief limp touch.

'No. I don't have my mother's talent.'

'Oh? What do you do?'

Ivy couldn't stop a grin from breaking out. She might look like a high-fashion model tonight, but… 'I work on a farm.'

Which, of course, meant she was of no account whatsoever, so she gave a nod of dismissal before she received one. 'If you'll excuse me, I've arrived a little late and my mother might be feeling anxious about it.'

'A farm?' Nonie Powell repeated incredulously.

'Let me help you find her,' Jordan said, moving swiftly and smoothly to hook his arm around Ivy's, pouring charm into a wicked smile. 'I'm very good at cutting a swathe through crowds.'

Ivy gaped at him in amazement while her heart started another wild jig. Did he pick up women as fast as that?

'Take care of my mother, will you, Henry?' he tossed at the gallery owner and they were off, Ivy's feet blindly moving in step with his as she tried to regather her wits.

'Kind of you,' she muttered, her senses bombarded

by the spicy cologne he was wearing, the hard muscular arm claiming her company, the confident purr of his sexy voice, the mischievous dance in his bedroom-blue eyes.

'Pure self-interest. We didn't get to talk much last time, and I'm bursting with curiosity about you.'

'Why?' she demanded, frowning over how directly he was coming on to her, even after she'd said straight-out she was a farm girl. Did that make her a novelty?

'The transformation for a start,' he answered teasingly.

She shrugged. 'My mother was not pleased with my appearance at that showing so I'm trying not to be a blot on her limelight again.'

'You could never be a blot with your shade of hair,' he declared. 'It's a beacon of glorious colour.'

He rolled the words out so glibly, Ivy couldn't really feel complimented. The playboy was playing and some deep-down sense of self-worth resented his game. She should be feeling happily flattered that Jordan Powell was attracted to her, delighted that her dress-up effort had paid off. Yet, despite the charismatic sexiness of the man, she was inwardly bridling against the ease with which he thought he could claim her company. Everything was too easy for him and she didn't like the idea of him finding her easy, too.

She halted in the midst of the gallery crowd, un-hooked her arm and turned to face him, her eyes fo-cussed on burning a hole through his to the facile mind behind them. 'Are you chatting me up?'

He looked surprised at the direct confrontation. Then amused. 'Yes and no,' he replied with a grin. 'I speak the absolute truth about your fabulous hair but I am...'

'I'm more than red hair,' she cut in, refusing to

respond to the heart-kicking grin. 'And since I've had it all my life, it's quite meaningless to me.'

Which should have dampened his ardour but didn't.

He laughed, and the lovely deep chuckle caressed all of Ivy's female hormones into vibrant life. Her thighs tensed, her stomach fluttered, her breasts tingled, and while her eyes still warred with the seductive twinkle in his, she was acutely aware of wanting to experience this man, regardless of knowing how short-term it would be. Nevertheless, resentment at his superficiality still simmered.

'Would you like me to rave on about your hair or how handsome you are?' she asked with lofty contempt. 'Is that the measure of you as a man?'

His mouth did its sensual little quirk. 'I stand corrected on how to chat you up. May I begin again?'

'Begin what?'

'Acquainting myself with the person you are.'

That was good. Really good. It hit the spot of prickling discontent. Nevertheless, Ivy couldn't bring herself to surrender to his charm without a further stand.

'Don't be deceived by this trendy get-up. It's for my mother. And Henry, who's a snob of the first order, not welcoming the common herd into his gallery. I'm simply not your type.'

He raised a wickedly arched eyebrow. 'Care to expound on what my type is?'

Careful, Ivy.

It was best for business not to reveal how she knew what she knew about him.

She cocked her head to the side consideringly and said, 'From what I observed last time we met, I'd say you specialise in beautiful trophy women.'

His brow creased thoughtfully. 'Perhaps they're the ones who throw themselves at me. Wealth is a drawcard so it's difficult to know if anyone actually likes you. It's more about what you can give them. I tend to sift through what's offered and...'

'May I point out it was *you* who grabbed me. *I* didn't throw myself at you.'

He smiled. 'Wonderfully refreshing, Ivy. Please allow me to learn more about you.'

It was impossible to muster up any more defences against that smile. Ivy sighed and gave in to the desire to have him at her side, at least for a little while. 'Well, my mother will be impressed if I have you in tow,' she muttered and curled her arm around his again. 'Lead on. Can you see her anywhere?'

He glanced around from his greater height, not that Ivy was short in these high-heeled platform shoes, but the top of her head was only level with his nose.

'To our right,' he directed. 'She's talking to a couple who appear interested in one of her paintings.'

'Then we mustn't interrupt, just hover nearby until she finishes with them and is free to notice me.'

'I think she'll notice you whether she's free or not,' Jordan said dryly.

Ivy didn't see anyone else in sequins. 'I hope I'm not too over the top in this outfit,' she said worriedly. 'The aim was to pleasantly surprise her with an up-to-date city version of me.'

'She didn't like the country version?'

Ivy rolled her eyes at him. 'When someone makes an art form of glamour, anything less offends their sensibilities, so no, she didn't care for my lack of care.'

'No problem tonight. You look as though you stepped right off the page of a fashion magazine.'

'I did.'

'Pardon?'

Ivy couldn't help laughing, her eyes twinkling at him as she explained. 'Saw a photo of these clothes, bought them, and hey presto! Even you're impressed!'

'You wear them well,' he said, amused by her amusement at her magic trick.

'Thank you. Then you don't think I'm over the top?'

'Not at all.'

She hugged his arm. 'Good! I've got you to protect me if my mother attacks.'

'I'm glad to be of use.'

He was a charmer. No doubt about that. Ivy was suddenly bubbling over with high spirits, despite knowing his track record with women. It wouldn't hurt to enjoy his company at the gallery, she decided. Much more fun than being on her own.

Her mother was dressed in a long flowing gown that fell from a beaded yoke in deepening shades of pink. Unlike Ivy, she wore pink beautifully, but then she wasn't like Ivy at all except for the curly hair. No one would pick them as mother and daughter. Sacha Thornton had grey eyes. Her hair was dark brown—almost black—and cascaded over her shoulders in a wild mane of ringlets, defying the fact she was nearing fifty. Though she didn't look it. Artful make-up gave her face the colour and vivacity of a much younger woman.

Bangles and rings flashed as her hands talked up the painting she was intent on selling to the couple. The expressive gesticulation halted in midair as Ivy—linked with Jordan Powell—moved into her line of vision. A startled look froze the animation of her face.

Ivy barely clamped down on the hysterical giggle

that threatened to erupt from her throat. She wished Heather was here to see the outcome of her pushing— first Henry, then Jordan Powell and now her mother totally agog. Heather would be dancing around and clapping her hands in wild triumph. And Ivy had to admit that even her tortured feet did not take the gleeful gloss off this moment.

It was ridiculous, of course.

All to do with image.

An image that didn't reflect who she was at all.

Nevertheless, she would happily wear it tonight for the sheer fun it was bringing her.

Her mother swiftly recovered, flashing an ingratiating smile at the prospective buyers. 'You must excuse me now.' She nodded towards Ivy. 'My daughter has just arrived.'

No hesitation whatsoever in acknowledging their relationship, nor in directing attention to her. The couple looked, their eyes widening at what they obviously saw as a power pair waiting in the wings. Jordan Powell was a splendid ornament on Ivy's arm.

'But please speak to Henry about the painting,' her mother went on. 'He's handling all the sales.'

She pressed their hands in a quick parting gesture and swept over to plant extravagant kisses on her daughter's cheeks in between extravagant cries of approval.

'Darling! How lovely you look! I'm so thrilled that you're here for me! And with Jordan!'

She stepped back to eye him coquettishly. 'I do hope this means you've come to buy more of my work.'

'Ivy and I came to greet you first, Sacha,' he answered, oozing his charm again. 'We haven't had a chance to see what's on show yet.'

'Well, if there's anything that takes your eye...'

They chatted for a few minutes, Ivy wryly reflecting that Jordan Powell was more important to her mother than she was. The man with the money. And the connections. She understood that this was what tonight was about for Sacha Thornton, not catching up with a daughter who didn't share the same interests anyway. At least she had succeeded in not being a drag on proceedings. The next telephone call from her mother should be quite pleasant.

'Ivy, dear, make sure Jordan sees everything,' her mother pleaded prettily when he was about to draw away.

'I'll do my best,' she answered obligingly. 'Good luck with the show, Sacha.'

'Sacha?' Jordan queried, eyeing her curiously as he steered her into the adjoining room which wasn't so crowded with people. 'You don't call her Mum?'

'No.' Ivy shrugged. 'Her choice. And I don't mind. Sacha never felt like a real mother to me. I was brought up by my father. That was her choice, too.'

'But you came for her tonight.'

'She always made the effort to come to events that were important to me.'

'Like what?'

'School concerts, graduation. Whenever I wanted both parents there for me.'

'Will you be staying the weekend with her?'

'No.'

'Why not?'

'Because I'd rather go home.'

'Which is where?'

'About a hundred kilometres from here.'

She wasn't about to identify her location to him. The

farm's website gave it away and he might have read it when he decided to use their service for his rose gifts.

'That's quite a drive late at night.'

'It won't be late. People drift out of here after a couple of hours.' She gave him an ironic grimace. 'You whisked me off before I could get a brochure detailing the paintings from Henry. Did he give you one?'

'Yes.' He took it out of his jacket pocket and handed it to her.

Ivy withdrew her arm from his and checked the numbers of the nearby paintings against the list in the brochure, determined on deflecting his physical effect on her. 'Right!' she said briskly, pointing to number fifteen. 'This is *Courtyard in Sunshine*. Do you like it?'

He folded his arms and considered it, obligingly falling in with her direction. 'Very pleasant but a bit too chocolate-boxy for me.'

Privately Ivy agreed, but the painting already had a red sticker on it indicating a sale, so somebody had liked it. 'Okay. Let's move on. Find something that does appeal to you.'

'Oh, I've already found that,' he drawled in a seductive tone, compelling Ivy to shoot a glance at him.

The bedroom-blue eyes had her targeted. It was like being hit by an explosion of sexual promise that fired up a host of primitive desires. She had lusted mildly over some movie stars, but in real life…this was a totally new and highly unsettling experience. She didn't even like this man…did she?

'You're wasting your time flirting with me,' she bluntly told him.

'There's nothing else I'd rather do,' he declared, grinning as though her rebuff delighted him.

Ivy huffed at his persistence. 'Well, if you must tag

along in my wake, you'll have to look properly at every painting or I'll lose patience with you.'

'If I buy one or two of them, will you have dinner with me?'

Had Ivy not been wearing such dangerous shoes, she would have stamped her foot. As it was, she glared at him in high dudgeon. 'That is the most incredibly offensive thing anyone has ever said to me!'

He actually looked taken aback by her attack. The dent in his confidence gave Ivy a wild rush of satisfaction. Jordan Powell wasn't going to find *her* easy.

He frowned. 'I thought it would please you to have your mother pleased tonight.'

'My mother has enough talent to draw buyers to her work or Henry wouldn't have it hanging in his gallery,' she retorted fiercely. 'She doesn't need me to sell myself to have a successful exhibition.' Her chin lifted in proud defiance of his obvious belief that anyone could be bought. 'I wouldn't do it anyway.'

He grimaced an apology. 'I didn't mean...'

'Oh, yes you did,' she cut in. 'I bet you think that all you have to do is offer your little goodies and any woman will fall in your lap.'

The grimace took on an ironic twist. 'I wouldn't call them *little* goodies.'

He might not have meant to put a sexual twist on those words, but Ivy felt her cheeks flame as an image of his naked body bloomed in her mind. 'I don't care how big they are,' she insisted vehemently. 'Why don't you go on back to *your* mother? I don't fit into your scene and never will.'

And having cut his feet out from under him, Ivy fully expected him to go. It would be the most sensible solution to the warring urge inside her to take what he was offering. Just to see, to know, to feel…

Which would inevitably end badly with her being discarded as he discarded all the rest.

# CHAPTER FOUR

JORDAN was faced with a decision he wasn't used to facing. No woman had ever told him to leave her alone. No woman had ever thrown so many negatives at him, either. Maybe Ivy Thornton wouldn't fit into his scene and he should walk away, stop wasting his time with her.

But he didn't *want* to walk away.

He liked her thorns.

They made her more intriguing, more challenging than the women in 'his scene'. And the fire-power coming from her incited visions of passion, lifting her desirability to virtually a must-have level. Just the sight of her had excited him. His fingertips itched to graze over every hidden part of her pale, almost translucent skin, not to mention stroking through the red-gold hair guarding her most intimate places.

Missing out on that...no.

He had to win her over.

'Never say never, Ivy. Things can change,' he said mildly, hoping to undermine her hard stance.

'I can't see that happening.' The fascinating green eyes flashed scepticism, but the tone of her voice was not so fierce.

'It was crass of me to link buying your mother's

paintings to my invitation to dinner and I apologise for the offence given,' he went on, projecting absolute sincerity. 'Please take it as a measure of how much I wanted you to accept, how much I wanted to spend more time with you.'

She frowned. After a few moments of cogitation, she gave him a narrow look that telegraphed he was on shaky ground, but her words granted him a second chance. 'Well, if you still want to accompany me around the gallery, I'll go that far with you.'

Triumph zinged through his mind. He only just managed to keep his smile appealingly rueful. 'I shall monitor my conversation with rigid regard to your sensibilities.'

It drew a laugh. 'I don't think you can hide your true colours, Jordan. Getting your own way must be habitual. You have all the tools to do it. Wealth, looks and charm to boot.'

He affected a helpless expression. 'None of which appear to carry any weight with you.'

She laughed again, shaking her head at him. 'I can't deny you're entertaining.'

He grinned. 'So are you, Ivy. I've just found a masochistic streak in myself. You can put me down as much as you like and I'll pop up for more.'

The green eyes sparkled. 'I might test that.'

He suddenly saw her in a black leather corselet, high-heeled boots laced up to her thighs, a whip in her hand. With her white skin and red hair, it made a fantastic vision. 'Are you a dominatrix?' he asked, seized by an irrepressible curiosity. He wasn't into that kind of kinky sex, but with Ivy might give it a try.

'A what?' She looked aghast.

'I thought you could have been suggesting it with

your "test" remark. Sorry. Had to ask. I do like to get my bearings with people, and you've completely knocked me off them.'

Her cheeks flamed again, the heat glow making her green eyes even greener. Her colouring was so entrancing, Jordan felt a considerable flow of heat himself though it was concentrated below the belt, not above it.

'I'm certainly not a dominatrix,' she stated emphatically.

'Good! Because I'm not really a masochist.' And he much preferred the idea of controlling the sexual games he played with Ivy, not the other way around.

She planted her hands on her hips. 'And just how did this conversation get to the bedroom? Do you have sex on your mind all the time?'

'Most men have sex on their minds most of the time,' he informed her with an ironic grimace.

'Do you think you can lift yours off it while we look at paintings?'

'Difficult with you dressed as you are, but I'll do my best.'

'Try hard.'

'I shall.' He whipped the brochure out of her hand, checked the number of the next painting and directed her attention to it. 'This one is called *Waterlilies*. Much more to my liking. Reminds me of Monet's great works. Have you ever been to Monet's garden at Giverny, Ivy?'

'No.'

'It's marvellous. Inspirational. After seeing what he created there, I was determined to bring something like it to every one of the retirement villages I've had con-

structed. There's nothing like a wonderful garden in
bloom to make people feel good. Best environment you
can have.'

The leap from sex to gardens was diverting but for Ivy
the damage was done. She couldn't lift her own mind
from thoughts of how he might be in the bedroom. He
had wonderful hands, long and elegant, and she couldn't
help imagining that their touch would be sensitive. Ben's
had never really been gentle enough. With him she had
often wished...though their relationship had been very
companionable and she might have married him if
he'd been more understanding during her father's last
months.

No chance of marriage with Jordan Powell.

Only bed and roses.

But the bed part might be an experience worth having.

Maybe she would never meet a man who would be
happy to share their lives. Ben had been the only possibility and she was already twenty-seven. For the past
two years there had been no one of any real interest on
her horizon. Jordan Powell was interesting, though not,
of course, in any lasting sense. But for a while...

It was tempting and becoming more tempting by the
minute.

He bought *Waterlilies*.

Henry put the red dot on the frame of the painting,
congratulated Jordan on a fine buy, smiled at Ivy as
though to say she had done well by her mother, and
moved off, probably hoping she would do more on the
sales front with a billionaire in tow.

'This was not a bribe, Ivy,' Jordan assured her. 'If
you weren't at my side, I would still have acquired it.'

'What will you do with it?' she demanded, wanting proof that his liking for it was genuine.

'Hang it in one of the nursing homes. It gives a sense of serenity. I'm sure the residents will enjoy it.'

Her curiosity was piqued. 'You seem to care about the people who buy into your properties.'

'I like them. They've reached an age where impressing a person like me is irrelevant. They say it how it is for them and I respect that.' There was a glint of cynicism in his eyes as he added, 'Honesty is a fairly rare commodity in my world.'

Yes, it probably was, Ivy thought, and wondered if the high turnover of women in his life was related to some form of deception on their part. Although that was putting them in the wrong and she shouldn't assume he was not. Undoubtedly Jordan Powell had his shortcomings when it came to relationships. She suspected he had a wandering eye, for a start. The last time she'd been in this gallery he'd sought an introduction to her when he was with another woman.

Sliding him a searching look, she asked, 'Are you honest yourself, Jordan?'

'I try to be,' he answered. The wicked twinkle reappeared. 'On the whole, I think I deliver whatever I promise.'

He was definitely thinking sinful pleasures.

Ivy's stomach fluttered in sinful excitement.

He cocked a challenging eyebrow. 'What about you?'

'Oh, I always deliver what I promise,' she said. The reputation of her business depended upon it.

'Ah! A woman of integrity.' He rolled the words out as though tasting them and his smile said he liked them.

Ivy was beginning to like him. She had managed to

keep her father at home where he'd wanted to be during the last months of his life, but if he had gone into a nursing home, one of Jordan Powell's would definitely have been the best choice. Sacha had done a painting of roses to hang in his bedroom, but her father would have liked *Waterlilies,* too.

A sudden welling up of sadness brought tears to her eyes. 'Let's move on. There might be something else that appeals to you,' she said huskily, turning aside to draw Jordan with her as she blinked rapidly and took a deep breath to restore her composure.

Gentle fingers stroked the hand resting on his arm. 'What is it, Ivy?' he asked caringly.

She shook her head, not wanting to explain.

'Something upset you,' he persisted. 'Was it my comment on integrity? Did you think I was being flippant? I assure you…'

'No.' She summoned up a wry little smile. 'Nothing to do with you, Jordan. I was thinking of my father.'

'What about him?' There was concern in the eyes that searched hers.

Ivy was touched by it. Her heart swelled with the sense of caring coming from him. Maybe he simply wanted to dispose of the distraction from him, get it out of the way so he could pull her back to what he wanted, but it tripped her into spilling the truth.

'Sacha's last show…when we first met here… It was soon after my father had died. Your mention of nursing homes reminded me of how hard it was for him at the end.'

'What did he die of, Ivy?'

'Cancer. Melanoma. He had red hair and fair skin like me and he was always having to get sun cancers removed. It made him fanatical about protecting my skin.'

Jordan nodded. 'So that's why you have no freckles.'

The comment made her laugh again. 'I'm a slave to block-out cream, hats and long sleeves. And you look like a slave to the sun—' with his gleaming olive skin, '—which should make you realise I definitely don't fit into your scene.'

He grinned. 'I have no objection to hats, long sleeves and particularly not to block-out cream. In fact, I think it would give me a lot of pleasure to spread it all over your beautiful skin. It would be criminal to have it marred in any way.'

Desire leapt between them—his to touch, hers to be touched. It simmered in his eyes and shot a bolt of heat through her bloodstream. Her pulse started to gallop. Ivy wrenched her gaze from his in sheer panic, riven with an acute awareness of feeling terribly vulnerable to what this man could do to her, for her, with her.

It would probably be a big mistake to let it happen.

She might end up wanting more of him than was sensible or practical, given his track record and her circumstances.

'What about a painting for yourself?' she rattled out, waving at the next section of the exhibition.

'Actually, I'm happy with the selection I have in my house,' he said, apparently content to follow her lead. For the moment.

Ivy was extremely conscious of him waiting, patient in his pursuit of a more intimate togetherness. It didn't need to be spoken. His intent was already under her skin, boring away at needs she had been dismissing for years. He'd brought the woman in her alive, kicking and screaming to be used, enjoyed, pleasured.

'I guess you have a collection of European masters,' she said lightly, thinking he could well afford it. She remembered Van Gogh's *Irises* had been bought by an Australian billionaire.

'No. I'm a proud Australian. I like my country and our culture. We have some great artists who've captured its uniqueness—Drysdale, Sydney Nolan, Pro Hart. I think I've bought the best of them.'

Sacha Thornton was not in that echelon of fame, although her work was popular and sold well. Ivy was impressed by the names he'd rolled out, impressed with his patriotism, as well. She'd never liked the snobbery of believing something bought overseas had a cachet that made it better than anything Australian.

'You're very lucky to have them to enjoy,' she remarked as they strolled on.

'It would be my pleasure to show them to you.'

She shot a teasing grin at him. 'I'd have to say that's one up on etchings.'

He grinned back. 'It's not a bribe.'

Her eyes merrily mocked him. 'Just holding out a persuasive titbit.'

'The choice is yours.'

'I might think about it,' she tossed at him airily, turning back to her mother's art.

He leaned close to her ear and murmured, 'You could think about it over dinner.'

The waft of his warm breath was like a tingling caress.

Temptation roared through her.

Fortunately two waiters descended on them, one offering a tray of hors d'oeuvres, the other presenting two glasses of fizzing champagne. 'Veuve Clicquot,' the drinks waiter informed them. 'Especially for you, Mr Powell. Compliments of…'

'Henry, of course. Thank him for me.' Jordan picked up the two glasses and held one out to Ivy who was busy choosing a crab tartlet and a pikelet loaded with smoked salmon and shallots.

'Hang on to it while I eat first,' she pleaded. 'I'm starving.'

'Then you need a proper meal,' he argued. 'If you like seafood, I know a place that does superb lobster.'

'Mmmh…' Superb lobster, superb works of art, superb Casanova?

The temptations were piling up, making Ivy think she really should throw her cap over the windmill for one mad night with this man.

She finished eating and took the glass of champagne he was holding for her. 'It's Friday night,' she reminded him. 'Wouldn't all the restaurants that serve superb meals be fully booked? How are you going to deliver on what you're promising?'

'There's not a maître d' in Sydney who wouldn't find a table for me,' he answered with supreme arrogance.

It niggled Ivy into a biting remark. 'And not a woman who would refuse you?'

The blue eyes warred with the daggers of distancing pride in hers. 'Please don't, Ivy,' he said with seductive softness. 'I haven't met anyone like you before.'

Her heart turned over. She'd never met anyone like him, either. 'The spice of novelty,' she muttered, mocking both of them—the strong desire to taste a different experience.

'Why not pursue it, at least for this evening?' he pressed persuasively.

She sipped the champagne, felt the fizz go to her head, promoting the urge to be reckless. 'All right,' she said slowly. 'You've sold me on the lobster. I will have dinner with you. If you can deliver what you promise,' she added in deliberate challenge, making the seafood the attraction.

It didn't dent his grin of confidence. 'Consider it done,' he said, whipping out his mobile telephone from a coat pocket.

A treacherous tingle of anticipation invaded Ivy's entire body. She didn't wait to hear him make arrangements, moving on to look at the few paintings they hadn't already seen, pretending it was irrelevant to her whether or not he secured a table for the promised dinner. Undoubtedly he would. Jordan Powell could probably buy his way into anything, any time at all.

But he couldn't buy her.

She would only go as far as *she* wanted to go with him.

One evening…maybe one night…

One step at a time, she told herself. He might turn her off him over dinner. The temptation could fizzle out. She couldn't remember the last time she had indulged her tastebuds with lobster. That, at least, was one pleasure she could allow herself without any concern over what was right or wrong.

# CHAPTER FIVE

THEY rode away from the gallery in Nonie Powell's chauffeured Rolls-Royce—borrowed briefly for the trip to the restaurant. Jordan's mother had rolled her eyes over the request, chided him for deserting her and given a long-suffering sigh as her gaze flicked over Ivy before waving them off, obviously resigned to her playboy son's weakness for a new attraction.

Ivy didn't care what his mother thought. Her own mother had been quite happy for her to leave with the billionaire, probably seeing him as the ultimate *city* man who might very well seduce her from country life. Ivy didn't care what Sacha thought, either. As far as she was concerned, this was simply an experience she wanted to dabble with while it was desirable.

When it stopped being desirable, she would take a taxi to her car and drive home. In the meantime, she was enjoying the experience of riding in a Rolls-Royce. She'd never done it before and it was most unlikely she would ever do it again. It felt luxurious. It smelled luxurious. She focussed her mind on memorising everything about it to tell Heather because it helped distract her from an acute awareness of the man sitting beside her.

He totally wrecked that mental exercise by reaching across, plucking her hand from her lap and stroking it with his long, elegant and highly sensual fingers. Her pulse bolted into overdrive. She found herself staring at their linked hands, fascinated by the juxtaposition of his olive skin and the extreme fairness of hers. She visualised them in bed together...naked...intertwined...black hair, red hair. The image was wickedly entrancing.

Ben's skin had been fair, though not as fair as hers. Jordan Powell was very different, in every sense. Was it the sheer contrast that made him so appealing? Why did being with him excite her so much? Was it the idea of living dangerously, which was not her usual style at all?

'What are you thinking?' he asked.

No way was she about to reveal those thoughts! 'Where are we going?' she countered, giving him a bright look of anticipation.

'Wherever you want to go,' he purred back at her, the sexy blue eyes inviting her to indulge any desire she had on her mind.

'I meant the restaurant,' she stated pointedly. 'My car is parked near the gallery. If I decide to walk out on you, which I might want to do, I'd prefer not to have a long journey back to it.'

He laughed, squeezing her hand as though asserting his possession of her even as he replied, 'Your escape route won't be a hardship. The restaurant is at Rose Bay. In fact, we're almost there.'

'Good! What's it called?'

'Pier. It specialises in seafood—spanner crab, lobster, tuna. I can recommend the trout carpaccio as a starter.'

'Then I hope you don't say anything offensive before we dine.'

'I'll watch my tongue,' he assured her, smiling as though he found her absolutely delicious.

Ivy immediately started wondering about how sexy his tongue was, in kissing as well as other intimate things. She had to wrench her gaze away from his mouth before he started guessing what she was thinking.

The idea of new experiences could be terribly beguiling.

It was another new experience to be welcomed so effusively into a classy restaurant, led to a table with a lovely view of Sydney Harbour, and given immediate smiling service. Obviously Jordan Powell was known to be a very generous tipper. Who could blame the average working person for bending over backwards to please him? Besides, he really was charming. To everyone! The maître d', the wine waiter, the food waiter, to her especially. Being in his company *was* an undeniable pleasure.

And the seafood was superb.

Especially the lobster, done simply in a lemon butter sauce.

Ivy sighed in satisfaction.

'Up to your expectations?' Jordan asked, his eyes twinkling pleasure in her pleasure.

'Best I've ever had,' she answered truthfully. 'Thank you.'

He gave her a slow, very sensual smile. 'I think the best is yet to come.'

Her stomach muscles contracted. Her mind jammed over what to do next—have a one-night fling with him or scoot for home. 'I couldn't fit in sweets, Jordan,' she said. 'Though coffee would be good.'

A glass of champagne at the gallery and a glass of chardonnay over dinner should not be affecting her judgement, yet she couldn't seem to manage any clear thinking with his eyes tempting her to stay with him and find out if he would deliver 'the best'. Maybe the coffee would sober her up enough to make the break, which, of course, was the most sensible thing to do. This whole thing with Jordan Powell was fantasy stuff. It wouldn't—couldn't—develop into a real relationship.

He ordered the coffee and handed his credit card to the waiter, indicating they would be leaving soon.

'I'll need to call a taxi to get back to my car,' Ivy quickly said. 'I can't walk that far in these killer shoes.'

'A taxi in twenty minutes,' Jordan instructed the waiter, apparently unperturbed about going along with her plan.

Twenty minutes later they left the restaurant.

A taxi was waiting for them.

It was only a short drive to where she had parked her car, but every minute of the trip shredded Ivy's nerves. Jordan had taken possession of her hand again and somehow she couldn't bring herself to snatch it free. Her heart was pounding. Her whole body felt on edge, fighting against the restrictions her mind was trying to impose on it. The pulse in her temples seemed to be thumping, *Go with it. Go with it. Go with it.*

The taxi stopped right beside her car.

Jordan released her hand, paid the driver, and was out, reaching back to help her alight on the kerb side of the street. Ivy finally teetered upright in the vertically challengingly high high heels and was fumbling in her handbag for her car keys when the taxi took off, leaving Jordan with her. Alone together. In the shadows of the night.

She scooped in a quick breath, desperate to relieve

the tightness in her chest. 'You should have kept it,' she said with an agitated wave at the departing taxi.

'A gentleman always sees a lady safely on her way,' he replied with mock gravity.

*With roses,* her mind snapped.

'I have to change my shoes,' she muttered, dropping her gaze from his, fighting the physical tug of the man. 'I can't drive in these.'

She pressed the Unlock button on her key fob and forced her legs to move, needing to open the trunk and get out her flat-heeled sandals.

'Let me help you take them off,' he said.

Those seductively sensual hands on her legs, her ankles, her feet... Ivy's mind reeled at how vulnerable she might be to his touch. 'I can manage,' she rattled out, reaching down to lift the lid of the trunk.

He intercepted the move, taking her hand, turning her towards him. She darted an anguished look of protest at him, caught burning purpose in his eyes, and suddenly her defences caved in, totally undermined by a chaotic craving to know what it would be like at least to be kissed by him.

'Ivy,' he murmured, stepping closer, sliding an arm around her waist. He lifted her hand to his shoulder, left it there and stroked her cheek, featherlight fingertips grazing slowly down to trace the line of her lips, his thumb hooking gently under her chin, tilting it up.

She was aware of weird little tremors running down her thighs, aware of her stomach fluttering with excitement, aware of her breasts yearning for contact with the hard wall of his chest, aware of the wanton desire to experience this man running completely out of control. He lowered his head. She stared at his mouth coming closer and closer to hers. She did nothing to stop him. It was as though all her common-sense mechanisms were paralysed.

His lips brushed hers, stirring a host of electric tingles. His tongue swept over them, soothing the acute sensitivity and teasing her mouth open. He began with a soft exploratory kiss, a tasting, not demanding a response but inevitably drawing it with tantalising little manoeuvres. Ivy couldn't resist tasting him right back, revelling in the sensual escalation that sent heat whooshing through her body.

The urge to feel him was equally irresistible. Her hand slid up around his neck, her fingers thrusting into his hair, loving its lush thickness. Perhaps it signalled her complete acquiescence to what was happening. Ivy was no longer thinking. Her mind was consumed with registering sensation, pleasure, excitement, the rampant desire to have her curiosity about Jordan Powell satisfied blotting out any other consideration.

His thumb glided along her jawline, caressed the lobe of her ear—an exquisite touch, moving slowly, sensually, under her hair to the nape of her neck. The arm around her waist scooped her into full body contact with him as his kissing became more demanding, less of an invitation, more an incitement to passion.

Ivy barely knew what she was doing. She loved being held so close to him, feeling the hard, male strength of his physique—the perfect complement to her highly aroused femininity. Excitement was flooding through her. Her mouth hungered for more and more passion from him, exulting in the deeply intimate aggression of his kisses. Never had she been so caught up in the moment. Never had she been driven to respond so wildly, so uninhibitedly.

She felt his hand clutch her bottom, pressing her more

tightly into contact with his sexuality. Her stomach contracted at the hard furrowing of his arousal. It should have been a warning to break away from him. Her body didn't want to. Her body wantonly rubbed itself against the blatant evidence of his excitement, exhilarated by it, madly bent on fanning this desire for her. It was wonderful to feel wanted again. She had been too long alone, and the woman inside her was craving connection—connection with this man, regardless of time and place and circumstances.

He swung her back against the trunk of the car, lifting her onto it, his mouth still ravishing hers as his hand burrowed under her mini-skirt, moved her silk panties aside, found the soft moist furrows of her sex and stroked her to a fever pitch of need, her whole being screaming for it to be fulfilled. Nothing else mattered. Nothing else existed for her.

It all happened so fast, the jolt when he plunged into her, the savage joy of it, the relief, the release of all nerve-tearing tension as her inner muscles convulsed and creamed around the marvellously deep penetration. And he repeated it, storming her with waves of ecstatic pleasure, pumping hard to the rhythm of his own need until he, too, reached the sweet chaos of climax.

She lay limply spreadeagled on the trunk of the car with him bent over her, the heat of his harsh breathing pulsing against her throat. If traffic had passed by them on the street, she hadn't heard or seen it. The night seemed to have wrapped them in a private cocoon, intensifying the feelings that still held her in thrall.

His arms burrowed underneath her, gathering her up. Amazingly her legs were wound around his hips and he supported them in place as he lifted her from the car and carried her to the passenger side, only relinquishing their intimate connection when he opened the door and lowered her to the seat. He kissed her while he fastened the safety belt, fetched the handbag she had dropped somewhere and laid it on her lap, kissed her again before closing the door and rounding the car to the driver's side.

She watched him in a daze—this virtual stranger with whom she'd shared such an erotically intimate experience. Languor was seeping into her bones. Somehow any action was beyond her. She barely grasped the fact that he had seized control of the situation, putting her in the car, retrieving her handbag and the car keys which he was now inserting in the ignition, having usurped her driver's seat. Her mind was stuck in one groove, endlessly repeating…

*I can't believe I did that.*

# CHAPTER SIX

JORDAN drove on automatic pilot, his mind still grappling with a loss of control which was totally uncharacteristic, especially in his relationships with women. He'd just acted like a randy teenage boy who couldn't wait to get his rocks off—a rampant bull, incapable of stopping. No sophistication. No finesse.

And worse! No thought of protection!

Shock billowed again.

He never took the risk of getting a woman pregnant. The possibility hadn't even entered his head. He'd wanted Ivy Thornton from the moment he'd seen her tonight, wanted her more and more with every minute they spent together, wanted her so much it was impossible to tolerate her driving away from him, but he'd meant to persuade, to seduce, to promise pleasure, not to...

'I can't believe I did that,' he muttered, shock tumbling into words he didn't mean to speak aloud.

He was still out of control.

'I can't, either.'

The shaky reply startled him into darting a glance at her. She wasn't looking at him. Her head was bent, the rippling fall of her glorious hair hiding most of her face. Her hands lay limply in her lap, palms upward, and she seemed to be staring down at them as though they didn't belong to her—hands that had gripped him in a fever of passion, inciting the wild act of intimacy they had both engaged in.

She was in shock, too.

Instinctively he reached across, took one of her hands, squeezed it. 'I'll make it better,' he said.

*Do it right,* he thought, which was why he'd put her in the car and was driving her to Balmoral—take her to bed with him and do all the things he'd imagined doing with her instead of succumbing to a mad rush of lust. It was too late to be worrying about protection now, not too late to enjoy all he wanted to enjoy with Ivy Thornton. Though he should check if she was using some form of contraception, know if there was a possibility of unwelcome consequences.

He frowned. It seemed crass to ask at this point. Besides, the damage was done if it was done. Using condoms for the rest of the night would be ridiculous. He might as well have the pleasure of totally unrestricted sex with her. It would be good. Great. Fantastic. He could bring up the issue later. She could take a morning-after pill if it was needed. Right now he wanted her riding with him, still caught up in what had happened between them.

It had been such an incredible rush—the excitement of her response, the mounting sense of urgency to seize the moment, take it as far as he could, her uninhibited complicity driving him to the edge, past it into plunging chaos. He couldn't remember ever feeling so exultantly *primitive.* Sex with Ivy had to be explored further. Much further.

'Where are you taking me?' she asked, her voice still slightly tremulous.

They were crossing the harbour bridge to the northern side of the city. He threw a reassuring smile at her, but her gaze was now fixed on the road ahead of them.

'I have a house at Balmoral. I'm taking you home with me,' he answered, hoping she was not about to protest the move.

She didn't.

She sat in motionless silence as he drove on over the bridge and took the turn to Military Road. Maybe she was having trouble putting thoughts together. Whatever...there were no stop signs coming from her and Jordan felt the buzz of anticipation shooting through his body again. He knew the desire was mutual. No doubt about it. It was only a matter of rekindling it, stoking the fire, making it a slow build-up of heat so the intensity didn't burn them out too fast.

He wanted the whole experience of Ivy Thornton.

A wham-bam on the trunk of a car was almost an insult to the fascinating woman she was.

He'd make it better for her.

A lot better.


Ivy's mind still felt as though it had been hit by a brick. Thoughts came slowly, as though emerging from a sea of molasses. She'd had sex with Jordan Powell. On the trunk of her car! He was driving her to his house at Balmoral. These were definite facts. She found it impossible to decide how she should be reacting to them.

Sex had never been like that for her...so compellingly reckless, so explosive, so erotically euphoric. Whether it was the man he was, the unusual set of circumstances, the long lack of any physical excitement in her life... Ivy couldn't quite put it together. He was a tempting devil and she had been tempted into going along with him, at the gallery, to the restaurant, and now to his home.

Why not?

Luck had blessed her in what could have been disastrous carelessness. She was in a safe week—no chance of falling pregnant. And it was too late to worry about sexual-health issues. Hopefully Jordan Powell was too fastidious a man to run those risks. Though he had done so tonight. Probably part of his shock at his behaviour.

Anyhow, she was problem-free and she hoped he was, too, because it was done now. She'd gone past the point of no return and finishing the night with him had a lot of appeal. How good a lover was he in bed? Could he give her an even more amazing experience? She'd never been inside a billionaire's house. It would be interesting to see how Jordan Powell lived, the paintings he had talked about, whether his bedroom had *playboy* stamped on all its furnishings.

Her car would be parked outside. She could leave whenever she chose to. This was an experience that was unlikely to ever come her way again and she wanted it. Yes, she did. Of course, it had to be limited. One night would satisfy her curiosity. She could allow herself that much. Any further involvement with Jordan would definitely not be sensible. Tomorrow she could leave with a smile on her face…knowing all she wanted to know.

Decision made.

Her mind moved on to working out how she should handle this new situation. It was hard to be cool and objective in these circumstances, having just shared such incredible intimacy with the man. Her nervous system was still buzzing. It seemed best simply to follow his lead. Unless his lead struck wrong chords, which wasn't likely with his well-practised charm. He'd done this with umpteen women. Though on the trunk of a car might have been a first, given his comment of disbelief. It was certainly a first for her.

All her inner muscles contracted with the memory of such intense pleasure. If Jordan could give it to her again…was she wicked to be wanting it? So what if she was! Did it matter just for once? Heather would undoubtedly say *go for it*. It wasn't as if she'd be hurting anyone. She was free to do as she liked.

Her gaze dropped to the hand still firmly linked to hers—a hand that knew how to touch, how to arouse overwhelming sensations, a tempting hand, a winning hand. But she was winning, too, wasn't she, being the object of its expert attention? She might never get to feel like this with any other man.

His fingers caressed her palm, making her skin tingle. 'Are you okay with this, Ivy?' he asked caringly, his deep rich voice washing over her thoughts.

'Yes, thank you,' she answered, wincing at sounding like a prim schoolgirl. The plain truth was she was not a *player*, not like him, and she didn't have any experience of acting like one. 'You can show me your paintings,' she quickly added, flashing him a smile to show she could be sophisticated about spending the night with him.

He laughed and squeezed her hand again. 'Your pleasure will be my pleasure.'

Which surely meant she should have a marvellous time with him. *Just relax and let it happen,* Ivy told herself.

He drove into a large paved courtyard fronting a very large white house with a double garage on the left and another double garage below an extended wing on the right. 'You have four cars?' Ivy asked as he parked hers adjacent to the very elegant portico framing the double front doors.

'Three,' he answered. 'The fourth space is taken up by Margaret's.'

'Who is Margaret?'

'My housekeeper. She lives in the apartment above the garage on the right, and Ray, my handyman and chauffeur, lives in the apartment above the garage on the left.'

Naturally he would need people to maintain such a luxurious property, as well as cater to his needs. 'How long have you had this place?' she asked, wondering if he really considered it his home or whether it was simply one of a string of residences.

'About five years. I like it here.' He flashed her a smile before alighting from the driver's side. 'I hope you'll like it, too.'

It didn't matter if she liked it or not, Ivy told herself, watching him round the bonnet to the passenger side, his mouth still curved in pleasure at having achieved his aim with her. She had her own aim, which was simply to satisfy her curiosity. And then leave. It would be really stupid to be seduced into staying more than one night with him, by what he had in his house or anything else. But when he opened her door and she stood up beside him she found her body still shaken to the core by his physical impact on her. It took gritty determination to keep her wits.

'My car keys,' she said, holding out her hand.

He gave them to her as he closed the door. She locked the car with the remote-control button and put the keys in her handbag. 'Lead on,' she invited, trying to adopt a nonchalant air, desperately hoping her jelly-like legs would firm up enough to allow her to walk with dignity in the perilous high-fashion shoes.

They didn't. She took one wobbly try and sat down on the steps leading up to the portico. 'I'm taking off these killer shoes right now,' she declared, bending over to unbuckle the straps.

'Let me help.'

In an instant he was crouching down in front of her, his strong fingers brushing her fumbling ones aside. He propped her foot on his bent knee for easier access and Ivy leaned back and let him do the job—much easier than doing it herself. And she let herself enjoy the way he caressed her ankles and massaged her toes when he'd freed them from all constriction.

'Better?' he asked, the blue eyes twinkling satisfaction in his handiwork.

'Yes. Thank you. Sorry about discarding the model image, but barefoot is more me,' she said flippantly, not wanting him to know she was craving a lot more of his touch.

'I'm happy for you to be comfortable with me,' he purred, kicking her heart into pounding at the thought of how comfortable they might get together.

She picked up her shoes, placed her feet firmly on the wide stone step and stood up. Which brought her virtually face to face with him because he stood on a lower step. Their eyes met. Raw desire in his. Ivy had no idea what he saw in hers, probably the naked truth of what she was feeling because she'd had no time to disguise it.

Instinctively she scooped in a quick breath. Then he was kissing her again and she couldn't help kissing him back. Her arms flung themselves around his neck, shoes and bag dangling from her hands. His arms crushed her into a fiercely possessive embrace. Excitement surged. She felt his erection furrowing her stomach, felt the moist rush of her own wild anticipation to experience him again. Her lower body automatically squirmed against his.

One hard muscular thigh pushed past hers, stepping up. He started arching her back, stopped, wrenched his mouth from hers. 'Must be out of my mind!' he muttered, shaking his head as though to clear it. His eyes blazed fierce determination. 'Come on, Ivy. We're going to do this in bed. In comfort!'

She'd completely lost it! Twice in one night! Passion-crazed!

Without his arm around her in support, she doubted her legs would have carried her to the front door. He swept her into the house with him. She didn't have the presence of mind to notice any decor details of the foyer. She saw nothing but the staircase in front of them. When they reached it her foot didn't lift high enough at the first step and she stumbled. He caught her before she fell, hoisted her up against his heaving chest and charged up the flight of stairs so fast he had to be taking them two at a time. It was like being rocked in a speeding train.

Ivy didn't notice anything else.

They landed on a bed.

'And we're not going to do this in the dark!' Jordan said, still in that tone of fierce determination. He reached across her and switched on a bedside light, but all she saw was his face hovering above hers, the strong masculine lines of it, the incredibly sensual mouth, the vivid blue eyes burning with wicked purpose, the black hair she had mussed with her fingers, the spiky look giving him a devilish aura.

*I'm a fallen woman,* she thought dizzily, but couldn't

bring herself to care, only too acutely aware that her body was willing her to fall all the way with Jordan Powell tonight.

'Let's get rid of these clothes,' he said, taking her shoes and handbag and tossing them on the floor, then straddling her thighs as he worked on removing her sequinned jacket, cami, bra, half-lifting her up from the pillow, laying her back down.

It was easy to be passive, let him do it, silently revelling in the glide of his hands on her naked skin. She didn't want to talk, only to feel. The bed linens were not linen. They were satin. Black satin. As befitted a playboy, she thought, but enjoyed the decadent sensuality of it for this time out of time.

He moved aside to strip off her skirt and panties— quick, deft actions—then paused to softly rake his fingers through her pubic hair, staring down at it as though fascinated, making Ivy wonder if the women he was usually with all had Brazilian waxes. She'd never had it done, only a bikini wax, and that only for indoor swimming. The sun was her enemy.

If her natural state turned him off…

'Amazing,' he murmured, and bent over to brush his mouth over the tight red-gold curls.

Definitely not a turn-off.

And the hot kisses he planted there were a nerve-jumping turn-on for Ivy. His tongue slid into the crevice between her thighs and teased her clitoris with mind-blowing delicacy—a tantalising tasting that generated an exquisite level of pleasure. It was all she could do to hold still. She wanted to focus on it, remember it forever. She forgot to breathe. Her whole being was concentrated on what he was doing to her. When he lifted his head, the trapped air in her lungs gushed out in a long, tremulous sigh.

'Don't move!' he commanded, placing a staying hand on her stomach. 'I want to feast my eyes on you while I undress.'

*Feast*...

He'd made her desperately hungry for him.

'You look incredible!' he said, his eyes glittering with awed excitement as they roved over her. 'Your skin... the pale creamy sheen of it...like the sheen of perfect pearls. And the red-gold blaze of your hair...what a brilliant contrast! The black pillow underneath it makes it even more vivid. You're a living work of art, Ivy. More fantastic than anything I've seen in a gallery.'

His admiration completely wiped out any build-up of angst about being viewed naked. Not that she had been fretting over it. They'd gone too far too fast for it to be a factor. And her attention was now totally fixed on him, watching the emergence of his naked physique as he stripped off his clothes.

He truly was a magnificent male—his body in perfect proportion to his height, muscular enough to be beautifully masculine without looking like a gym junkie obsessed with weight-lifting. The darker tone of his olive skin gleamed with good health. The sprinkle of black hair across his chest arrowed down in a narrow line, provocatively pointing to the impressive evidence of his sexual arousal.

He certainly didn't disappoint on the physical front. Ivy's inner muscles quivered at the sight of him. Her hands itched to touch, her breasts yearned to feel his weight on her, her arms and legs buzzed in anticipation of curling around him, holding all that male power, feeling it. She had never known such compelling, urgent lust for a man.

But when he came to her, he caught her reaching hands and held them above her head. He lay beside her with one strong thigh slung across both of hers, locking them down. 'I want to taste all of you, Ivy,' he said, his hotly simmering gaze dropping to her breasts.

Her breath caught in her throat as he dipped his head and circled one aureole with his tongue, causing her nipple to harden further into a taut bullet. She closed her eyes and concentrated on the wild flow of sensations as he licked and sucked. He was so good at it, soft and slow, flicking, lashing, drawing her flesh into his mouth at just the right strength. It was so blissful, her back instinctively arched, inviting him to do more, take more.

She slithered her hands out of his grasp, wanting, needing to touch him, to stroke his hair, to glide her fingers over his back, to press him closer, imprint all of him on her memory. She felt his flesh flinch under her caresses and smiled, knowing he found it erotic, glad she excited him as much as he excited her.

'Can't wait,' he muttered, jerking up to change position, swiftly inserting his leg between hers.

*At last,* she thought exultantly, moving just as swiftly to accommodate him, to give him achingly ready access for the intimacy she craved. A wave of ecstatic satisfaction swept through her as he thrust inward, filling the yearning core of her need. She fiercely embraced him, her legs goading him into a hectic rhythm, harder, faster, deeper, revelling in the explosive action, feeling it drive her closer and closer to the exquisite splintering chaos of intense pleasure he had given her earlier tonight.

He took her there again.

With even more shattering intensity.

Ivy heard herself cry out at the incredible peak of tension before it broke, flooding her with a tsunami of sweet sensation. Some loud unintelligible sound broke from his throat, too, and he collapsed on top of her, breathing hard. She hugged him tightly, wallowing in the possessiveness of the moment, loving him for the gift of this marvellous experience.

He rolled onto his side, carrying her with him, hugging her just as tightly. Her head was tucked under his chin. He kissed her hair, rubbing his mouth over it as though he had to taste that, too. Ivy felt drained of all energy, yet beautifully replete. *A perfect feast,* she thought contentedly. It had been right to give in to temptation. She would never forget this as long as she lived.

He started stroking her back, lovely, long, skin-tingling caresses. She sighed with pleasure. He knew exactly how to touch a woman. She wished she could always have a lover like him. It was a pity a relationship with him wouldn't last, but Ivy was not about to fool herself on that score. She was a temporary episode in the life of Jordan Powell, and it was best for her to cut it short and not get too attached to him.

One night.

That was what she had decided.

It was a very sensible decision—one she would definitely keep.

'This time we are going to do it nice and slow, Ivy,' he said in a tone of determined purpose.

She smiled, wondering if it annoyed him that he hadn't managed to completely control the pace. She stirred herself enough to say, 'I liked it fine the way it was, but carry on as you like.'

If he wanted to do more, she was not about to object.

The night was still young.

She was happy to pack as much into it as he was capable of giving her.

# CHAPTER SEVEN

IVY'S BODY-CLOCK WOKE her at six. It was her usual rising time at the farm. Still feeling tired from the night's unusual activities, she could have easily gone back to sleep, but looking at the man lying beside her—the absolutely yummy and extremely seductive man—she decided this was the time to leave, before he woke up and used his very persuasive powers on her to stay with him for the weekend.

Which would be terribly tempting.

However, she was half in love with him already. What woman wouldn't be after the night they had just spent together? Any longer with him would be getting in too deep and being dumped when he'd had his fill of her could hurt a lot. Better for her to do the dumping right now.

Her curiosity about him had certainly been satisfied. She hadn't seen much of the house he lived in but that was relatively unimportant. Her gaze roved quickly around the bedroom as she eased herself off the bed. Everything was black and white, like the en suite bathroom she had visited during the night.

There were two paintings on the walls she hadn't noticed before—both of them from Sydney Nolan's Ned Kelly series. It seemed a strange choice to have the legendary Australian bushranger on display in his bedroom. Ivy had imagined there'd be something more erotic—nude scenes or whatever—but the black frames and the famous black armour Ned Kelly had worn did suit the decor.

The thick white carpet muffled any sound her footsteps might have made on her way to the bathroom. Very quietly she closed the door and had a quick wash. A black silk wrap-around robe hung from a hook near the shower. She borrowed it to wear down to the car—easier than redressing in the sequinned stuff, which she could put in the trunk where her normal clothes for driving were stowed. A quick change into them and she would be on her way.

Jordan was still sound asleep as she swept up her high-fashion gear and underclothes from the floor. Having crept out of the bedroom and closed the door on the scene of her surrender to temptation, she found herself on an inside balcony overlooking the foyer. It was easy to spot the staircase. She was bolting down it when a woman emerged from a room to the left of the foyer— smallish, grey-haired, wearing a white uniform.

They both halted in surprise at seeing each other.

The woman looked Ivy up and down, the expression on her face clearly saying, Here's a new one.

It had to be the housekeeper, Ivy thought, trying to fight a hot tide of embarrassment.

'Good morning,' the woman said. 'I'm Margaret Partridge, Jordan's cook and housekeeper. You can call me Margaret. We don't stand on ceremony here.'

'Hello,' Ivy blurted out, grateful for the matter-of-fact tone of the other woman's greeting though her heart was still thumping madly over being discovered in the act of doing a runner. 'I'm Ivy...Ivy Thornton. I...uh...need to get some day clothes out of my car.'

'I'll unlock the front door for you,' Margaret said obligingly, moving to do so. 'I was just on my way to the kitchen. Would you like a cup of coffee? Jordan rarely rises before nine on a Saturday morning so there's no need to hurry over anything.'

'Thank you, but I won't wait. I have to get home,' Ivy explained in a rush, quickly resuming her descent to the foyer.

Margaret's eyebrows lifted quizzically. It was probably something else new to have one of Jordan Powell's women leave his bed before he did. Ivy was super-conscious of the housekeeper's firsthand knowledge of her employer's affairs. The flush she hadn't been able to stop was burning fiercely on her cheeks as she walked briskly to the opened front door.

'I'm happy to cook you breakfast before you set off,' Margaret offered, obviously curious about her.

'That's very kind.' Ivy managed a polite smile. 'But it's only an hour's drive. I'll eat at home.'

'You should have coffee before you go. It will perk you up for the drive. I'll make it while you dress and have it ready for you in the kitchen.'

The uncritical manner of the housekeeper did ease some of Ivy's embarrassment. Nevertheless, while there might be no danger of Jordan waking up any time soon, the situation was too uncomfortable for her to delay her departure any longer than she had to.

'You probably don't know where the kitchen is,' Margaret ran on. 'Last door on your right at the back of the foyer leads into the breakfast room. You walk through it to the kitchen. And there's a powder room under the staircase where you can change if you don't want to go back upstairs.'

'Right! Thank you,' Ivy said firmly, not committing herself to anything though she welcomed the information about the powder room. The handyman/chauffeur might be roaming around outside the house.

'There's no need to hurry,' Margaret repeated, apparently sensing Ivy's urge to bolt and wanting to reassure her that time wasn't a problem.

Which might be true, but Ivy still didn't want to risk having a clean escape foiled.

The housekeeper left the front door open for her. Ivy made a quick trip to her car, unlocked the trunk, dumped the clothes she was carrying, grabbed the blue jeans, white top and flat navy sandals, and was back inside the house with the door closed within a few minutes. The powder room was smaller than Jordan's en suite bathroom but just as classy in grey and white and silver. Having dressed in her casual clothes and plaited the messy cloud of her hair, she looked for a hook to hang the black robe on. There wasn't one. After dithering for several moments, she folded it up neatly and placed it on the vanity bench.

The seductive aroma of freshly brewed coffee hit her as she stepped out of the powder room. Again she dithered, aware it would be very rude to the helpful housekeeper to simply walk out without acknowledging her efforts to please. It was also very ill-mannered not to thank Jordan for the pleasure he had given her last night. Being dumped without a word was really quite nasty.

Deciding to risk staying a couple of more minutes, she followed Margaret's directions to the breakfast room, which had such a fantastic view it momentarily stopped her. Beyond a wall of glass, a tiled patio surrounded a glorious blue swimming pool. Past that was the harbour, sparkling in the early-morning sunshine and already busy with water traffic.

Her gaze quickly swivelled around to take in the whole room. White tiles on the floor were largely covered by a beautiful thick rug in shades of blue and aqua. On this stood a glass-topped table surrounded by white leather chairs. Two Pro Hart paintings dominated the back wall—bushland scenes with vivid blue skies. This was how a billionaire enjoyed breakfast, she thought, pushing herself on to the kitchen.

It, also, was predominantly white and with the same view as the breakfast room. A quick glance around from the doorway revealed an extremely professional set-up with top-of-the-range appliances which would have seduced a master chef—a dream working area for any cook.

The housekeeper was pouring freshly brewed coffee into a mug. She smiled a welcome at Ivy and waved her to the stools on one side of an island bench. 'Milk? Cream? Sugar?' she inquired.

'Please excuse me. I can't stay. I must get home,' Ivy said firmly. 'I've left Jordan's robe in the powder room. I hope you won't mind returning it for me.'

'Is there some emergency?' Margaret cut in with a frown of concern.

'I just have to go,' Ivy replied, not wanting to be drawn into conversation. 'I'd be grateful if you'd tell Jordan from me...thank you for the lovely night.'

Margaret nodded slowly. 'All right. I'll pass that on.'

Ivy flashed a smile of relief. 'Thanks again for everything. Bye now.'

A quick wave of her hand and she was on her way out of Jordan Powell's life, satisfied she had left with some grace.

Jordan was conscious of a sweet sense of well-being as he drifted up from sleep. Memory clicked in. Ivy. He opened his eyes, his mouth already curving into a smile. It was a jolt to find her gone from his bed, a further jolt to see her clothes were no longer on the floor. He darted a glance at the clock—8:27 a.m.

Maybe she was an early riser. People who worked on farms usually were. Margaret was always up early, too. Possibly she was giving Ivy breakfast. Feeling an urgent need to check, Jordan hurtled off the bed and strode to the bathroom.

His black robe was not on its peg.

It brought the smile back to his face.

Ivy would look very fetching in it with her glorious hair.

Feeling more confident of her presence in his home, Jordan had a quick shower, shaved, grabbed another black robe from his dressing room and went downstairs with a bounce of happy anticipation in his step. He actually grinned as he wondered what Margaret thought of Ivy—very different to his usual run of dates, and both women were quite direct in saying what was on their minds, nothing evasive or deceptive about either of them.

No one in the breakfast room.

Jordan frowned as he strode through it, not hearing any conversation coming from the kitchen and the door to it was open. He found Margaret sitting at the island bench—alone—sipping a mug of coffee.

'Where's Ivy?' he snapped.

Margaret viewed him with sharp interest as she delivered her answer. 'Gone. And you needn't speak to me in that tone of voice, Jordan. I did try to keep her here. Offered her breakfast. Pressed her to have a cup of coffee, but she wouldn't have it. Nothing was going to make her stay. She was determined to leave.'

'Did she tell you why?' he shot at her, his mind too fraught with disappointment to monitor his voice tone.

'No. But she did ask me to thank you for the lovely night. I must say she had beautiful manners, unlike some of the other women you've dated.'

Jordan burned with frustration. Never had a woman left him before he wanted her to, and for it to be Ivy... no, he could not, would not respect her decision to reject what they could have together. She had been with him all the way last night, and *lovely* fell far short of what had happened between them.

A hard, cynical thought flashed into his mind. Was this some deliberate move to test how keen he was to have her in his life? A clever power game? Being the only one who didn't throw herself at him had worked to hold his interest last night. Running off might be the goad for him to give chase.

A billionaire would be a great catch for a farm girl.

Except the billionaire had no intention of being caught.

But he did want more of Ivy Thornton. A lot more. And he could not believe she didn't want more of him. So he would give chase, ensuring their connection would only end when *he* wanted it to end.

'Did she tell you where she was going?'

'Home.'

He grimaced with impatience at the short reply. 'Can

you be more specific, Margaret? I know Ivy works on a farm, but I don't know its location.'

'An hour's drive from here, she said.'

He threw up his hands. 'Too vague!'

'Sorry. I can't help on that point. If you want my opinion, I think she was deeply embarrassed at being found in your home and couldn't get out fast enough. Very different to others I might mention who were positively smug about being here with you. And since she didn't give you any contact details, it doesn't look like she wants you to pursue her.'

He frowned. Maybe this wasn't a calculated move. Margaret was very good at reading character. Possibly Ivy was shocked at herself. He'd taken advantage of her shock last night, sweeping her along with him. But she'd been fine in his bed. Fantastic in his bed! However, if she wasn't used to having sex with a man on a first date...was she ashamed of herself for crossing some moral standard?

Which might mean...oh, hell! If she was a *good girl,* not on any contraceptive pill...he'd totally ignored that issue last night, deciding to deal with it later. If taking that risk had hit her this morning...if there was a very real possibility she had fallen pregnant...she might have been overwhelmed by a sense of panic.

'I have to find her, Margaret.' He started tramping around the kitchen, raking his hair in agitation. 'I have to!' It wasn't just the pregnancy question, he couldn't tolerate the idea of never seeing Ivy again, never having her again.

'Not that it's any of my business,' Margaret said with an air of making it hers this once. 'But it's my observation that you're not into having serious relationships with women, Jordan, and Ivy Thornton didn't strike me as a sophisticated playgirl. It might be a kindness to respect her decision and let her go. Simply write her off as the one that got away.'

'No! No!' The emphatic negatives exploded off his tongue. He glared at Margaret, who looked stunned by the explosiveness of his reaction. 'I can't!' he added decisively, not wanting to explain why. 'I have to find her,' he repeated in teeth-gritting determination.

'And then what?' Margaret asked, critical brown eyes putting him on the spot, holding judgement on his motives.

Ruthless purpose swept straight past the uncertainties in his mind. 'Then she can tell me to my face that she doesn't want anything more to do with me.'

Ivy wouldn't be able to do it, not with any honesty.

'Fair enough,' Margaret conceded. 'What would you like for breakfast this morning?'

She slid off her stool, ready to get down to business.

Jordan was infuriated by her matter-of-fact dismissal of his intense frustration with the situation. And breakfast was the last thing he wanted to consider right now. He shook a finger at her and fiercely declared, 'Ivy Thornton is not going to be the one who got away!'

Margaret stopped and stared at him as though he'd suddenly metamorphosed into a stranger. 'Sorry if I spoke out of turn,' she said with uncharacteristic meekness. 'It was just...I liked her, Jordan. And I wouldn't like it if you hunted her down and hurt her.'

'I have no intention of hurting her.'

Margaret pressed her lips together, buttoning up against offending him with any further comment, but her eyes definitely challenged him to keep that stated intention. He would be the lesser man in her estimation if he didn't.

Ivy had clearly made a more strongly positive impression on her than any of the other women he'd brought here.

'I like her, too, Margaret,' he said more quietly. 'Very much.'

She nodded, still tight-lipped.

He sighed.

Battle lines were drawn.

He now had to win over Ivy—and make her happy to be with him—in order to win over Margaret or he'd be getting burnt breakfasts. Possibly even worse! She might walk out on him, too!

A burst of adrenaline raised his fighting instincts.

Jordan was not a man to back down from a challenge.

One way or another, he'd have what he wanted!

# CHAPTER EIGHT

IVY kept telling herself she'd been absolutely right to get out of Jordan Powell's life, but her body was still fired up by the memory of him, and it was quite impossible to get him out of her head. Being home on the farm didn't really help. She couldn't stop imagining how it might have been if she'd spent the weekend with him in his beautiful Balmoral home.

It was a hot morning and shaping up to be an even hotter day. A quick dip in his gorgeous swimming pool would have been lovely, not to mention...

The ringing of the telephone was a welcome distraction. She dived on the receiver, hoping the caller would ground her in real life again. No such luck! It was her mother, who instantly recalled everything about last night.

'Ivy, I've just had Jordan Powell on the line.'

Her heart kicked into overdrive. 'What did he want?' she asked, her voice uncharacteristically shrill. With fear or excitement?

'Well, I thought it was rather odd. You did go out with him last night and you looked as though you were enjoying his company, but since you obviously didn't give him your address...was that an oversight, dear, or don't you want to see him again?'

A bomb of anxiety exploded in her mind. 'Did you tell him where I lived?'

'No. He was very charming. Always is. But I thought I'd better check with you first.'

Relief poured through Ivy. She didn't have to face Jordan again, didn't have to battle against her attraction to him. Her decision to leave had definitely been right and it was much easier to hold on to it from a distance. This call proved how shaky her resolution could be, given his immediate presence.

'I'm glad you did,' she said in a calmer tone. 'He's not for me. Good for a night out, but I'd rather leave it there.'

'Are you sure, dear?'

'I'm sure. Thank you for protecting my privacy. I really appreciate it. And congratulations on the show. Lots of sales last night.'

'Yes. Very gratifying. And it was lovely to see you looking so stunning, Ivy. Living right up to your full potential. I felt so proud of you.'

It was a nice feeling to have pleased her mother. Ivy relaxed enough to smile as she remarked, 'Well, I didn't want to let you down again and it felt really good when Henry's jaw dropped at seeing me. He's such a snob!'

'But he's very adept at wooing the right crowd at his gallery, dear, bringing in people with the money to buy. It's a pity I have to disappoint a good client like Jordan Powell...' She sighed. 'Are you absolutely certain you wouldn't like to see him again, Ivy?'

'Yes, I am. I don't fit into his kind of life and he wouldn't fit into mine. End of story,' she said emphatically, ignoring the flutters in her stomach and forcefully remembering the way Jordan's housekeeper had checked her over—the latest candidate for her employer's bed.

'Well, in that case, my lips are sealed. Such a shame!' Sacha muttered and disconnected.

By Monday morning Ivy was more settled into the idea that her night with Jordan was a one-off experience which she could look back on with pleasure and no regrets. Heather, of course, wanted to know everything, the moment she swept into the office.

'Did he zero in on you?'

'Yes, he did,' Ivy answered, and even managed to smile at her friend's whoop of triumphant excitement.

'Tell me all!' Heather demanded.

Ivy confessed that she had succumbed to the temptation of enjoying Jordan's company at the gallery and described the follow-up dinner date in great detail, much to Heather's salacious enjoyment.

'And then? Did you go and look at his paintings?'

'Some of them,' Ivy teased. No way was she going to confide what actually led to the trip to Balmoral! Some things were too intensely private.

'If you came straight home after that, I'll kill you!' Heather ranted. 'I want to know if he's a fantastic lover.'

Ivy laughed, needing to keep the whole episode light and unimportant. 'He is. I'd have to say he's very, very good at sex. I'm glad I stayed the night.'

'Only the one night?'

'That was enough, Heather. You know he's a playboy. I left while he was still asleep and ran into his housekeeper on my way out. If you'd seen the way she looked at me…'

'Another notch on his bedpost?' Heather interpreted with a sympathetic grimace.

'It didn't feel good. I was glad I skipped out when I did.'

'Fair enough!' Heather grinned. 'Marvellous that he

was great in bed, though. I think you needed to be taken down from the shelf and dusted off. Hopefully it will get you more interested in looking for some real action in your life.'

'I shall hope for it,' Ivy replied, grateful that Heather had already relegated the experience with Jordan Powell to the realm of fantasy. Where it belonged. 'Now let's get down to work.'

Occasionally, throughout the day, Heather questioned her further, but it was mainly curiosity about the Balmoral house, what Ivy had seen of it, nothing really personal. Orders for roses came in. The courier was loaded up and sent to the designated addresses. By late afternoon, Ivy was satisfied that her brief encounter with Jordan Powell had been dealt with and would quickly slip into the past. A memory. Nothing more.

Until he struck again!

'Uh-oh!' Heather muttered and swung her computer chair around to face Ivy, rolling her eyes for dramatic effect. 'You're not going to like this!'

'What?'

'Jordan Powell is ordering roses and double chocolate fudge to go to your mother.'

'My mother!'

'With a message attached. For you, Ivy.'

For one gut-twisting moment, she thought he knew the rose farm was hers.

'It says… "Please tell Ivy…"'

No, he was still trying to get to her through her mother!

The relief was so intense she didn't hear what the message was.

'Say that again, Heather?'

'"Please tell Ivy I need to talk to her. I'll be at the

Bacio Coffee Shop under the clock in the Queen Victoria building between noon and two o'clock on Saturday and Sunday. I'll wait until she comes."'

He wanted a face-to-face meeting, counting on his charm to win her over to what *he* wanted. She wasn't going to risk it. No way! She might fall victim to it again.

'What do you want me to do?' Heather asked.

'Put the order through. It's business as usual. I'll speak to my mother about it.'

'Okay.'

But it wasn't *okay*. The same order came through on Tuesday and Wednesday and Thursday and Friday, constantly reminding Ivy of the man.

'Maybe you should go and talk to him,' Heather said as she was leaving on Friday.

'No!' Ivy answered firmly.

But her weekend was totally wrecked, thinking about him waiting for her, wondering if he had something to say she would actually want to hear. Which was ridiculous, given his track record with women.

He didn't give up.

The order was repeated on Monday and every day of the next week. Her mother complained she was drowning in roses and putting on weight with all the double chocolate fudge.

'You don't have to eat it,' Ivy cried in sheer frustration with Jordan's determined campaign. 'Give it away. Give the roses away.'

'I don't see why you can't go and talk to him,' her mother argued. 'It's not as if he's asking you to come into his parlour, Ivy. It's a public place. You can walk away any time you like.'

'I don't want to see him. Full stop.'

However, her refusal to meet Jordan did not stop him.

Her mother was inundated with roses and fudge for the third week running. Even Heather, with all her Rose Valentino knowledge, started doubting Ivy's decision.

'You must have made a big impact on him, Ivy. To be this persistent…and waiting two hours at a coffee shop for you to turn up…' She frowned and shook her head. 'I don't think a dilettante would do that.' Her eyes gathered a look of fantastic possibilities as she added, 'What if it's a serious attraction? Maybe you should give it a chance. You did say he was a great lover.'

'How could it work between us? I'm here. He's there,' Ivy pointed out with considerable vehemence, needing to hang on to common sense.

'Distance wouldn't be a problem for a billionaire. He probably owns a helicopter.'

'I bet it's no more than an ego thing and I'm not giving in to it,' Ivy declared with fierce determination.

Heather said no more, keeping her thoughts to herself, but Ivy could see the glint of pro-Jordan speculation in her eyes as the orders continued through the fourth week. Which was downright persecution!

Heather no longer supported her stance.

Her mother was ranting and raving.

On the fourth Saturday morning after Ivy had walked out of Jordan Powell's life, she decided she had to meet him and give him a piece of her mind—an angry, outraged, totally damning piece which would rock him back on his billionaire-playboy socks and make him leave her alone!

She braided her hair back into one thick plait, minimising its impact. Blue jeans, a royal-blue T-shirt and navy sandals helped give her a fairly nondescript appearance. Without any make-up she was satisfied that

Jordan would not find her particularly attractive today. It had to be impressed upon him that he was wasting his time with her.

She drove to Sydney and used the parking station under the Queen Victoria Building, which was expensive but handy for a quick getaway. The big clock inside the shopping mall was showing ten minutes past midday as she kept herself inconspicuous amongst the crowd of shoppers passing by the tables belonging to the Bacio Coffee Shop. They were set out in open view, most of them occupied by people wanting a lunch break.

Her heart kicked into a gallop when she spotted Jordan at one of them, a pen in hand, apparently working on a crossword in the newspaper spread out on his table. He wasn't looking out for her, but he was there all right, all set up to wait patiently for her arrival. The relentless pressure for this meeting sent a bolt of panic through Ivy, quickening her pace as she walked straight past where he was sitting, too agitated by the sight of him to be in control of this encounter. Her righteous anger had just been swallowed up by a scary sense of vulnerability.

She stopped at a safe distance and turned to watch him surreptitiously. The back view of him was not so nerve-joltingly handsome, but it was impossible to set aside the fact she had gone to bed with this man, knew his body intimately, had run her fingers through his thick black hair, nestled her face contentedly into the curve of his neck and shoulder—sharp memories raising a terribly acute sexual awareness, both of him and herself. The moment she looked into his bedroom-blue eyes she would see them there, too, and how was she going to ignore or dismiss that once she sat down with him?

Ivy dithered, the need to stop Jordan from inserting himself into her life losing all its furious momentum in the power of his presence. She saw other women glancing at him from nearby tables, probably wishing they could catch his attention. Even though he seemed oblivious of their interest, he still had the charismatic magnetism to draw theirs. It kept tugging at her, too. Coming here had been a mistake—a big mistake.

He would stop sending the roses eventually.

She didn't have to say or do anything.

Except tear her gaze away from him and go back home.

*So go,* she told herself, but before she could bring herself to act, Jordan's head jerked up as though reacting to something. He rose swiftly to his feet, turned, shooting a questioning gaze around his vicinity. Ivy froze, couldn't move a muscle, the certainty of no escape now seizing her mind, making another encounter with him inevitable.

He saw her. The smile that instantly spread across his face turned her insides to mush. It wasn't a smile of triumph, more one of sparkling pleasure, inviting her to share it—share all the things that had pleasured them both. He lifted a hand in an open gesture of welcome, encouraging her to join him at his table.

Her heart started pumping again. Hard. She wondered if he would chase her if she turned and ran. But there was no dignity in that. Besides, she wasn't sure her wobbly legs were capable of racing anywhere. Somehow she had to firm up her mind—as well as the rest of her body—and directly address the situation with Jordan Powell.

She concentrated on forcing her feet forward and putting a glowering expression of reproach on her face, smiting his treacherous smile as she made her way to his table. He held out a chair for her. She sat down. He quickly folded the newspaper and slipped it under his chair as he resumed his seat, the blue eyes more serious now, appealing for her patience.

'It's good to see you, Ivy,' he rolled out in his deep, sexy voice.

'I only came to stop you from pestering my mother,' she declared, keeping her face tight with disapproval.

He leaned forward, elbows on the table, speaking with quiet urgency. 'I had to talk to you. The night we spent together…I didn't use any protection and I didn't ask if you were on the pill. I've been worried that you might have fallen pregnant.'

'Oh!' Her chest loosened up as her lungs expelled a gush of air in a sigh of relief. This was reasonable. It wasn't a mad pursuit of her. In fact, it was really nice of him to care about serious consequences from their mutual recklessness. 'It's okay,' she assured him. 'That was a safe time for me. You don't have to worry any more.'

'A safe time?' he queried, frowning as though he didn't quite understand.

'In my monthly cycle,' she explained.

'You don't normally use any contraceptive device?'

He sounded incredulous, as though any woman in her right mind shouldn't be protecting herself against *accidents*. Undoubtedly the women he mixed with did.

She leaned forward to make her position very plain, flushing with the violence of her feelings on his fly-by-night attitude. 'I told you I wasn't your type. I told you I wouldn't fit into your scene. I don't do sex on a casual basis and I haven't been in a relationship for over two years so I have no reason to be always ready.'

'Ah!' A smile of satisfaction tugged at the corners of his mouth. 'Then I'm glad you found me as irresistible as I found you. Which is the second thing I want to talk to you about.'

Ivy rolled her eyes and sagged back in her chair, feeling under attack again. 'Haven't I made my point, Jordan?' she cried in exasperation.

'No. Because it's based on assumptions about me which I don't think are fair,' he argued.

They weren't assumptions. His orders to the rose farm provided hard evidence of how he conducted his sexual affairs. However, she couldn't lay that out to him without revealing how she had such inside knowledge and she didn't want to give him any more information about herself. 'You're a notorious playboy,' she said accusingly, folding her arms in defensive belligerence.

He grimaced. 'Because of what I am, who I am, a lot of women throw themselves at me, Ivy. I wouldn't be human if I didn't find some of them attractive. Unlike you, they're intent on making themselves attractive to me, but the effort wears thin after a while. Their real selves emerge.' He shook his head as he ruefully added, 'And it's never what I want.'

'What do you want?' she asked, privately conceding what he said could be true. A handsome billionaire would be a target for most women.

The blue eyes burned into hers. 'Honesty,' he said, which he'd previously told her was the rarest commodity in his world.

Maybe it was. The more Ivy thought about it, the more she could see this could be a real downside in being obscenely wealthy...people cosying up to him for what they could get out of being close to big money. She didn't need what he had. Being happy in her own world, she didn't covet his kind of life at all. The only thing missing for her was…a loving husband, family, a shared future.

She couldn't see Jordan Powell in that picture.

Though she certainly wouldn't mind sharing her bed with him.

No denying that.

Her entire body was humming with tempting memories and sympathy for his situation with other women was sneaking into her heart, undermining her resistance to the strong attraction of the man.

'Well, I want honesty, too, Jordan,' she said, struggling to maintain a defensive line. 'Why don't you admit I was nothing more than an amusing challenge to you on the night of my mother's exhibition? Someone different to play with. And you simply didn't like it when I finished the game before you did.'

'Not a game, Ivy.' He shook his head over her choice of words. His mouth quirked ironically. 'A game doesn't spin out of control as that night did.'

The trunk of the car…the front steps of his house… her vaginal muscles contracted sharply at the pointed recollection of control being totally lost.

'That has never happened to me before,' he added quietly. 'Which does make you different, Ivy. Not in an amusing sense. In a very unique sense. And you've just told me it was extraordinary for you, too. So I don't think we should walk away from it. I think it's something we should explore a lot further. Together. With honesty. No game-playing.'

There was no trace of glib charm in his voice, no seductive twinkle in the blue eyes boring into hers. He looked completely serious, sincere, emitting a forceful energy that silently attacked and demolished any argument against what he was proposing.

Ivy suddenly found herself thinking of her parents. They'd led separate lives for as long as she could remember, but they'd never divorced and had always shared a bedroom when they'd spent weekends together. They'd each pursued their own interests, respecting the needs that drove them to take different paths while still maintaining an affectionate bond.

It wasn't what she wanted for herself.

But what if there was nothing better?

Never would be anything better.

She stared at Jordan Powell and knew she wanted more of him. Whatever that meant...wherever it led... she did want to explore how much they could have together.

# CHAPTER NINE

JORDAN concentrated fiercely on willing Ivy to agree.
The idea that she had been playing a power game with
him had been whittled away by the sheer length of time
it had taken her to respond to his message. Her attitude
today—everything about her—indicated that inspiring
a chase had not been the intent behind absenting herself
from his life. She was fighting the attraction between
them with all her willpower.

Or was all this a clever act, designed to draw him
more firmly into her female net?

She *had* turned up.

And was forcing him to argue for a chance with
her.

Throw out the challenge…hook the man like he'd
never been hooked before!

Her fascinating green eyes had savaged him, mocked
him, transmitted hard unyielding judgement, but now
they were strangely blank, focussed inward, giving no
sign of what she was thinking.

He couldn't deny his many affairs—most of them
very short-lived. Ivy had plenty of reason to believe she
would be no more than a brief addition to the long list.
It could actually turn out that way. He wasn't about to
promise it wouldn't. How could he know, at this stage,

how long the attraction would last, whether familiarity would eventually breed contempt, as it so often had with other women?

All he knew was his gut was in knots, waiting for her reply. And that hadn't happened before. None of it had…sensing her presence before he even saw her, the mule-kick to his heart when his instincts had proved correct, the intense flare of desire which owed nothing to her outward appearance which was obviously meant to express lack of interest in him.

He *was* hooked.

But that didn't mean he was caught.

The instant zing between them told him she wasn't immune to what they had shared. He had to tap into that again, make her want what he wanted. Regardless of what was going on in her mind, Jordan was determined on drawing her into *his* net. Even more so now that she was here with him.

'Would you like a cup of coffee while you think about it?' he asked, intent on forcing her into active communication.

The blank shield on her eyes snapped open to reveal deep wells of vulnerability—a host of fears swirling through wishful possibilities. 'Yes,' she said huskily, sucking in a quick breath to firm up her voice. 'Cappucino, please.'

He signalled a waitress, ordered two coffees and a plate of toasted sandwiches to tempt Ivy into eating. There was nothing like sharing food to put people more at ease with their company, and it seemed—from the wildly swimming look in her eyes—that Ivy was wound up in an emotional dilemma about becoming more involved with him.

Unless she was a brilliant actress.

He was reminded of what Margaret had said...*I wouldn't like it if you hunted her down and hurt her.*

He had hunted her, with good reason, Jordan told himself. Nevertheless, being hurt by him could be high on the list of fears in Ivy's mind. A playboy...

To him it was a pragmatic lifestyle, given his circumstances. He was quite happy going along for a ride, hated the idea of being taken for one. He was beginning to think this was a different situation with Ivy, more a journey of discovery than the usual ride.

Her lashes had swept down, hiding her thoughts again. He leaned forward, pressing for her attention. 'Ivy, you're not a trophy woman to me.'

The green eyes flashed wildly amused sparks at him as she burst into a peal of laughter. 'Anyone seeing us together today would think you had rocks in your head to consider me one, Jordan.'

He relaxed into a laugh himself. 'Which proves my point. I want your company, regardless of trappings.'

'Mmmh...' She cocked her head consideringly. 'I'd have to say I enjoyed your company, too. Though I'm not sure how well that would wear over time. I don't think we have much in common.'

Oh, yes they did! Fantastic sex together. Unforgettably fantastic!

Maybe she read that thought in his eyes. A tide of heat whooshed up her neck and burned her cheeks. She wriggled in her chair, probably discomforted by an attack of hormones charged-up with the same memories he had. He had to shift a bit himself to accommodate his own charged up anatomy. If they weren't in a public place... but the sex hadn't kept her with him last time. He had to make more inroads into her psyche.

He tried a disarming smile. 'I like it that you don't see *me* as a trophy.'

That was a good, testing line.

She shot it down in flames, instantly firing derision at it. 'Too tarnished by a lot of careless wear.'

'I care about you,' he shot back at her, throwing all cynical caution aside. 'We have something special going between us. Too special to dismiss. I've never waited for a woman as I've waited for you. And don't tell me you don't feel it, too, because you do, Ivy. This is *us* and it's not like anything in the past. Face it. Give it a chance. It might be the best thing either of us could ever have.'

*A chance...*

Yes.

Ivy's whole body yearned to feel again the pleasure he could give her and the intensity he was transmitting made his arguments too persuasive for her to fight any further. It *had* been special. Unique for her as well as him. Of course there was no guarantee it would last but what guarantee could be attached to any relationship these days?

'How do you see it working?' she blurted out.

He leaned forward eagerly. 'We could start with weekends. This weekend.'

Her heart instantly kicked into a gallop. She hadn't come ready for this. 'I didn't bring anything with me. And I'm still not on the pill.'

'You don't need anything. I don't want to share you with anyone. Not today or tomorrow. And I'll take care of protection while you're arranging your own.'

Panic seized her. This decision felt too rushed. 'You forgot last time.'

'I promise you, I won't forget again.'

No, he wouldn't, not after being worried about getting her pregnant. Having a child with her was not on his agenda. It might never be. She had to think of this as a trial period and not get too…too…stuck on him. He'd been a playboy for so long, it was best if she didn't let herself believe their affair might turn out any different to his previous relationships. All she was committing herself to was giving it a chance.

She eyed him with fierce intensity. 'Don't send me any roses. Ever!'

'Sending them to your mother did bring us back together. It got the right result, Ivy,' he reminded her seriously.

'I don't mean *them!*' she said in emphatic dismissal. 'I mean the roses you send as a matter of rote to all the women who have held your interest for a while.'

He frowned, puzzled by her knowledge of intimate details of his past affairs.

Ivy gritted her teeth and revealed the truth. 'You order them from me, Jordan. It's my rose farm you deal with over the Internet. From this moment on, I'm writing you off as a client. When it's over with me and you find someone else, find yourself another rose source. Okay?'

He looked totally gobsmacked.

Ivy didn't care. Involving herself with Jordan meant there was no way of continuing to hide her business and she simply couldn't bear the idea of him resuming his Rose Valentino modus operandi with other women in the future. Not through her farm anyway.

The waitress arrived at their table with their coffees and the plate of toasted sandwiches. Ivy was too churned up to eat anything but she was grateful for the coffee. It was hot and sweet and strong and her shredded nerves needed soothing. She sipped it, covertly watching Jordan gradually recover from his shock and wondering how he would react to her revelation.

It was actually a good test of his feelings towards her. He wanted honesty. She'd just laid it out to him. He didn't reach for a sandwich or his coffee. He sat completely still, eyes lowered, a pensive expression on his face, probably reflecting on how much business he'd done with her farm over the years.

'I see,' he finally murmured, an ironic tilt to his perfectly sculptured mouth. Twin blue laser beams targeted Ivy's eyes. 'I now understand how sceptical you must have been over my intentions and how reluctant you still are to get involved with me. But you're here thinking about it, and I'm here fighting for a chance with you because we connected so strongly we'd always wonder what might have been if we didn't pursue it. That's the truth of it, isn't it, Ivy? The honest truth.'

'For me, yes,' she answered, her own mouth quirking with irony as she added, 'Where you're concerned, it requires a leap of faith I'm not sure I can make.'

He nodded. 'Make it. Take the risk. It's worth a try.' He flashed her a dazzling smile. 'Remember how good it was. Think how good it can be again.'

She hoped it would be, because the decision was already made. The buzz of anticipation was in her blood and she was no longer physically capable of backing away from this man.

He made a flip-flop gesture, unsure of where she was at. 'You can always end it if I let you down.'

She smiled, her eyes mocking the off-hand offer. 'I don't think you're too good at accepting an end you don't want, Jordan. My mother can testify to that.'

'But I hadn't let you down, Ivy,' he reminded her. 'You just assumed I would. Let's be fair now.'

She laughed, giddy with the sense of taking an even more dangerous step with this man. 'Okay. I promise I'll be fair.'

One black eyebrow arched in appeal. 'No harking back to my past?'

'I'll take you as I find you until you do let me down.'

'Done!' His hand smacked down on the table in triumphant satisfaction as he rose from his chair, emitting an electric energy that sent Ivy's pulse zooming into overdrive. 'Take me to wherever you've parked your car,' he commanded, his eyes blazing with the desire to move her with him to a far less public place.

The car...images of wild sex bloomed in Ivy's mind, flustering her into a hot flush. She waved at the plate of sandwiches in a rush of agitation. 'What about this?'

'Not what I'm hungry for. Are you?'

'No.' Impossible to eat anything with lustful thoughts running riot and there was no point in delaying what she'd decided to do. 'You haven't paid,' she said, trying to sound in some control of herself as she pushed up from her chair.

He took out his wallet, removed a fifty-dollar note, anchored it on the table under the sugar bowl, then reached for her hand. She gave it to him, consciously feeling every sensation of his touch: the power of the fingers entwining hers, the tingling pleasure from the rub of his flesh, the seductive caress of his thumb. Why he, of all men, could evoke this acute sexual excitement in her, she didn't know, but strangely enough it was a relief to simply surrender to it.

'The elevator,' she directed. 'Level two of the basement car park.'

They walked together, moving like an arrow of purpose that could not be diverted. The crowd of shoppers milled around them, no one blocking their path even minimally. Ivy was barely aware of other people. The connection to the man beside her virtually obliterated everything else.

Worries wormed their way through her mind. Had she given in too easily? Was she a fool for giving in at all? Were there other things she could have said, should have said before letting him lead her back into his life? Was there any real possibility of a relationship with Jordan developing into something solid?

Yet…did any of that matter when he could make her feel like this?

They reached the elevator just as its doors opened. A family—mother, father, child in a pram—stepped out, an ordinary family, what Ivy had hoped to have herself. Nothing with Jordan was going to be ordinary. Was she totally mad to involve herself with him?

They moved into the elevator. No one followed them. Jordan pressed the button for L2. The doors closed. They were alone together in the small compartment. Jordan erupted into action, scooping her into his embrace, kissing her with a hunger that found an instant, overwhelming response. Weeks—a whole month of repression burst under a wild surge of need to taste him again, feel him again, have him stoke the excitement that made everything else irrelevant.

Their mouths meshed in feverish passion. Their hands seized, travelled, pressed, dragged, dug in, feeding the fierce desire to take possession. They were so immersed in each other, they didn't notice the elevator coming to a halt, its doors sliding open.

'Sorry to interrupt you guys, but…'

The voice brought them back to earth with a heart-thumping shock.

'Right,' Jordan muttered, and swept Ivy past the amused onlooker into the cavernous car park.

Her legs were wobbly. She tried to catch a breath, get her wits in order, orientate herself enough to find her car. 'Where's yours?' she asked.

'My what?'

He looked as distracted as she felt. 'Your car.'

He shook his head. 'Didn't bring one. Had Ray drop me off.'

'Who's Ray?'

He stopped, sucked in a deep breath, obviously re-gathering himself as he turned to face her, lightly grasping her upper arms, the blue eyes boring into hers, his voice gruff with emotion. 'Are you okay, Ivy? You're not about to do another runner on me?'

'No.' Tearing herself away from him now was un-thinkable. She wanted him too much. When or if he let her down…somehow she would deal with the fallout. Until then…she summoned up a shaky smile. 'Though let's not lose our heads again. At least, not here.'

His smile poured out relief and reassurance. 'I can wait a bit longer. And to answer your question, Ray is my handyman and he'll drive in to pick me up at two o'clock if not instructed otherwise. We can be home before he leaves if we go in your car.'

'Okay.' She opened her shoulder-bag to get out the keys. 'It's probably better if you drive. You're more fa-miliar with the route to Balmoral.' Besides which, it was doubtful she could concentrate on the road.

He released her arms to take the keys, dryly commenting, 'It will make it easier to keep my hands off you.'

She laughed, giddily light-hearted with the tense burden of decision lifted. A quick glance around located her car and she hooked her arm around his to haul him in the right direction. 'This way. And we both need to exercise some care, Jordan.'

'Don't worry. I *will* take care of you, Ivy. In every sense there is.'

That was a big promise. Ivy wasn't sure she believed it. But she was willing to take this journey with him. It was probably an *Alice in Wonderland* kind of adventure and one day she would wake up from it. She hoped she would be able to treasure the good, shake off the bad and remember it as a risk that had been worth taking.

# CHAPTER TEN

AT the first red traffic light Jordan whipped out his mobile phone, making a quick call to his handyman who promptly answered.

'No need to come, Ray. I'm heading home now in Ivy's car. Would you please tell Margaret it will be dinner for two tonight. Maybe a late lunch, as well.'

'Will do. And...uh...congratulations, boss.'

'Thanks, Ray,' Jordan said dryly, aware that his campaign to make contact with Ivy was well known to his household staff, with conflicting degrees of support. Ray had been rooting for him to win while Margaret reserved judgement on the outcome.

He closed the phone and slid it back into his shirt pocket, throwing a glance at Ivy to check all was well with her before turning his attention back to the bank-up of traffic waiting for the light to change. 'Why are you frowning?' he asked, wanting to wipe the tense expression from her face.

She heaved a sigh and shot him an anxious look. 'Your housekeeper...I guess she's seen a lot of women come and go in your life, Jordan. It's just kind of embarrassing. I know I shouldn't care what she thinks, but...'

'Don't worry.' He grinned as he reached across and

gave her hand a quick reassuring squeeze. 'Margaret likes you. In fact, I have a strong suspicion I'll be damned to perdition if I don't treat you right.'

'How could she like me?' Ivy queried in amazement. 'I only spoke to her for a few minutes. And that was when...well, it was obvious I'd spent the night with you.'

'Oh, I got the blame for that...having my wicked way with a nice girl.'

'How does she know I'm a nice girl?'

'According to Margaret, you have beautiful manners. Believe me, as long as you treat her with respect, you'll get the same respect back. Respect and honesty are Margaret's prime standards. Cross those lines and you're in her black books. An honest bit of sex between a man and a woman does not worry her one bit. Okay?'

Ivy relaxed, a happy relief in her smile. 'Okay. She sounds like quite a character.'

'She is. Hiring her was one of the best decisions I've ever made.'

And Jordan had the strong feeling that pursuing Ivy had been one of his best decisions, too.

The car behind them honked—a warning that the light had turned green and the traffic was moving again. Satisfied that he'd removed any fretting from Ivy's mind, Jordan drove on, revelling in the anticipation of having her to himself for the rest of the weekend, which gave him plenty of time to sort out any other concerns she might have about being involved with him.

It was highly vexing to find his sister's silver Porsche parked in the driveway of his Balmoral home. Apart from the fact that he didn't want any visitors taking his attention away from Ivy, Olivia was a self-centred snob whose manner could be very off-putting to anyone who wasn't used to her. Besides, she wouldn't be here unless she wanted him to *fix* something for her, which meant she'd want his undivided attention.

'Damn!' he muttered as he brought Ivy's car to a halt behind the Porsche.

'You have a visitor?' Ivy enquired, a wary look on her face.

'My sister, who only drops in on me when she has some problem to unload, so I won't be able to get rid of her until I hear her out.'

'If it's a private problem, Jordan, she won't want a stranger listening in.'

'No, she won't.' He grimaced an apologetic appeal. 'Would you mind very much chatting to Margaret while I deal with it? I'll ask her to make you some lunch. Or you could browse through the newspaper. I'm sorry. This is an awkward start, not what I...'

'It's okay,' she quickly assured him. 'Family should come first, especially if there's a problem.'

He heaved a sigh of frustration. 'Olivia makes trouble for herself. My father spoiled her terribly...his little princess. Don't be upset if she's dismissive of you. It won't be personal. She'll just be so full of herself, no one else counts.'

The green eyes filled with wry self-mockery. 'Well, I don't count for anything in her life.'

'You do in mine,' he said emphatically, feeling the question mark over his involvement with her and hating it. He turned in his seat to reach out and cup her cheek, his eyes boring into hers with forceful intensity. 'You do in mine, Ivy. Give me time and I'll prove that to you.'

He kissed her, wanting their desire for each other to obliterate everything else, leave no room for doubts. Excitement surged through him at her fierce response.

She didn't want to doubt him. She wanted to lose herself in the same passion he felt. It was hell having to restrain himself to a kiss when he was so hungry for her. He mentally cursed his sister for being an obstacle to the rampant urge to sweep Ivy straight up to his bedroom. A month of waiting and still he had to wait.

'Later,' he promised, breathing the word against her lips as he forced himself to break the kiss. 'You have to meet my sister now, Ivy.'

'Yes,' she whispered huskily.

He had to fight down his reluctance to separate himself from her, move away. It took an act of will to curb the rebellious needs of his body and alight from the car, taking the steps demanded by Olivia's unwelcome presence in his home. Ivy swayed a little as he helped her from the passenger seat. He tucked her arm around his for the walk inside, governed by the strong instinct to support and protect his woman.

*His...*

Strange...he couldn't remember feeling actually possessive of a woman before. Probably it was the long waiting that had made him uncertain of having Ivy again. And *that* was yet to happen. Olivia had better behave herself, he thought grimly. If she gave Ivy any cause to skip out on him...

'There you are!'

The words were flung at him the moment he and Ivy entered the foyer—Olivia emerging from the lounge, a highball glass in hand, obviously in a state of intoxication, her usual perfect grooming having taken a slide today: eye make-up smudged, her shoulder-length hair dishevelled, silk blouse crumpled, linen trousers badly creased.

She had the same blue eyes and black hair he did.

Tall and voluptuously curved, she could and usually did make a striking impact on people, but she was not about to make a good impression on Ivy at this meeting. He closed the front door behind him, eyeing his sister with stern displeasure. Getting drunk didn't fix anything, and driving a car while over the alcohol limit was downright irresponsible, let alone illegal. Not acknowledging Ivy's presence and addressing him as though he'd put her out by his absence was more than he could tolerate.

'Why are you here, Olivia?' he threw back at her.

She ignored the question, eyeing Ivy up and down with a supercilious look on her face. 'Who is this? Taking up with Cinderellas now, are you, Jordan? Been through the whole socialite pack?'

'Keep a civil tongue or go,' he said cuttingly. 'I don't have any patience for your rudeness today.'

'Sorry. I just haven't seen her before,' she rolled out with a shrug. 'Will I recognise the name?'

'Ivy. Ivy Thornton. Unfortunately, I have no pleasure at all in introducing you, Olivia.'

'Tough!' She sneered. 'I'm family and you can't get rid of family. The good old tie of blood is always there. Whereas Ivy...no doubt she will turn into Poison Ivy in due course. They invariably do, don't they?'

She was right, but due course hadn't been run yet, and he wasn't about to let Olivia spark off another bout of resistance from Ivy when he'd just brought her to the starting line. 'You've been warned!' he threw at his sister, stepping back to open front door. 'I'll call Ray to drive you home.'

'Oh, for pity's sake! Why take offence when you carry on about being honest and calling a spade a spade?' She flicked another look down her nose at Ivy. 'I have to concede you have the good sense not to marry any of them. I, on the other hand...' The jeering spite suddenly crumpled into tears and the eyes she turned back to Jordan were wretched pools of despair. '...was fool enough to hitch myself to a sleazy, cheating scumbag who plans on blackmailing me for all I'm worth.'

'Blackmail?' This was serious business. Jordan frowned over it as he quietly closed the door again. 'What does your husband have to blackmail you with, Olivia?'

Her *third* husband, who fell in the toy-boy range—twenty-three years old to her thirty-four—sweet, loveable Ashton whose gym-toned body promised sex on legs and had obviously delivered it beyond the marriage bed, which had always been predictable. But what had Olivia done to put herself in a blackmailing situation?

She shook her head, choking out words between sobs and shuddering intakes of breath. 'You've got to help me, Jordan. You've got to. Daddy would have fixed it.'

Jordan gritted his teeth. His father had always freed his darling daughter from the consequences of her follies, which, of course, meant Olivia had never learnt any hard lessons from experience. His own upbringing had been designed to teach him the strong hand required to run a business empire, to anticipate the consequences of any decision and make careful provision for them before acting.

Although well aware of why Olivia was the way she was, he was sorely tempted to let her stew in her own juices this time, make her count the cost for once, but blackmail was a dirty criminal act, and he couldn't allow anyone to stick his sister with it. Nevertheless, some lessons had to be hammered home right now.

'Okay, you want something from me, Olivia. I want something from you,' he said in a hard relentless tone, totally unsympathetic to her blubbering tears in the face of the insults she had flung at Ivy—a woman she didn't know and didn't care about knowing—putting his win at risk.

'What?' Olivia asked sulkily.

'Firstly you will apologise to Ivy for your ignorant remarks about her. Take a deep breath now and do it with some grace, please, or you can take your trouble to the cemetery and tell it to Dad's tombstone.'

Her jaw dropped in shock. She goggled at him and then at Ivy who hadn't said a word, despite the nastiness that had been directed at her. God only knew what she was thinking! Probably that any connection with him was fast losing its desire-power!

'Sorry,' Olivia finally mumbled at Ivy in a woebegone fashion. 'I'm just so upset. I wanted you to go so I could have Jordan to myself. I...I shouldn't have said those things.' She dashed the tears from her eyes with her hand, lifted her chin and looked belligerently at Jordan. 'Is that enough?'

'No, but it will do for the present. The next time you meet Ivy, you'd better take the trouble to make her acquaintance in a decent fashion. You could learn good manners from her for a start.'

'All right! All right!' She snapped, throwing up her free hand, then dropping it into a plea for him to stop browbeating her. 'I'm sorry. Okay?'

'None of this is okay, Olivia. Go back into the lounge and wait for me. Don't drink another drop of alcohol. If you have a serious problem we need to talk about it seriously. Soberly. Without any more theatrics. I'll take Ivy to Margaret, who I'm sure will make her feel more comfortable, and I'll bring you some strong black coffee.'

She flounced off into the lounge, slamming the door behind her in protest at being treated to some discipline instead of oodles of indulgence. Jordan reined in the angry resentment stirred by the whole scene with Olivia and turned quickly to draw Ivy into his embrace, searching her eyes for reactions to it, anxious to erase any damage done.

'I apologise for my sister's behaviour. It's beyond my control, Ivy. She just lashes out indiscriminately when she's upset. Not that that's any excuse...'

To his intense relief she gave him an ironic little smile. 'I thought you did a fairly impressive job of taking control.'

He heaved a rueful sigh. 'My parents spoiled Olivia rotten. All she had to do was throw a tantrum and she was given anything she wanted. It used to drive me around the bend. Still does. But she could be in real trouble with this blackmail business. I'll have to deal with it.'

'Of course you do,' she said sympathetically, reaching up to smooth the frown from his brow. 'What your sister said to me doesn't matter, Jordan. I know I'm not a Cinderella and I've never been poisonous to anyone. It seems to me it's your family wealth that's the poison.'

True, but...he needed to find out how profitable Ivy's rose farm was, whether it was on shaky ground, check that she wasn't a Cinderella in hiding as Biancha had been, because he knew only too well that it was the Cinderellas of both sexes who brought poison to his family's wealth.

'It does attract con-artists and fortune-hunters and Olivia invariably falls for them,' he replied with an unguarded touch of bitterness.

'That must be really nasty for her when she finds out she's been fooled.'

Being fooled was always nasty. Only once had he fallen into that trap, and not even the promise of fantastic sex forever would blinker his eyes to it again.

'It's about time she exercised some judgement,' he said grimly. 'At least testing the waters before blindly wading in.'

'Like you do?'

Her eyes reflected a mental reviewing of his many brief affairs in a different light. Not so much the playboy but the billionaire with a cynical part of his brain alert to anything false.

'Ivy, we can continue this conversation later. We should move on now. I don't trust Olivia not to hit the bottle again.'

'Yes. Better get the coffee coming.'

He was grateful for her quick understanding. No selfishness, no sulky pouts at being put aside for a while, just a fair assessment of the situation and a reasonable reaction to it. He liked her all the more for it. He hoped she spoke the truth about not being a Cinderella.

They found Margaret in the kitchen. As usual, she had anticipated what would be needed and already had the coffee brewing. Margaret was no fool. She was always aware of everything in this household. Regardless of her former reservations about his pursuit of Ivy, she welcomed her with a smile and instantly offered to take care of her needs, too. The Saturday newspaper was spread out on the island bench, the travel section uppermost, and Ivy slid straight onto a stool, obviously prepared to wait for him and acquaint herself with his housekeeper.

Feeling sure that this issue was settled, Jordan switched

his mind to dealing with Olivia and her problem. She was pacing around the lounge in nervous agitation—thankfully without a glass in her hand—when he took in the coffee, advising her to sit down, sip it and compose herself.

He waited until she did so, quelling his own impatience to get on with it, knowing that calm, cool deliberation had to be brought to damage control. He seated himself on the armchair adjacent to the sofa where Olivia had flung herself and thought about how to counter a blackmail threat until his sister could not contain herself any longer.

Having taken one sip of coffee, she threw a look of angst at him and blurted out, 'He's got a video of me having sex with him and he's going to post it on the Internet if I don't pay up.'

'Did you agree to the video or did he film it without your permission?'

Her gaze dropped. She plucked at her trousers. 'I... uh...thought it was fun at the time. Something...intimate...to watch together.'

Jordan shook his head. How many girls and women fell into that trap, letting their boyfriends take naked shots of them, only to find the photographs were not kept private—were posted on the Internet or flashed around on mobile phones? It was rotten behaviour by the guys, but with today's technology at everyone's fingertips, the women should wise up to the risk of being put out there.

'It's happening all the time, Olivia,' he said, exasperated by her foolishness. 'Why not tell him to publish and be damned? There's nothing shameful about having sex with your husband.'

'But anyone can look at it,' she cried, appalled at his

solution. 'It's humiliating, Jordan. I can't bear the idea of lots of people having a peepshow of me.'

'You've got a great body. You don't mind showing it off. You won't be the first heiress who's had to weather baring all on the Internet,' he said dismissively. And just maybe she'd be wiser next time around.

She grimaced and muttered, 'It's not just that.'

'Then stop pussyfooting around and give me the real dirt, Olivia.'

She erupted from the sofa, throwing up her hands, flouncing around to avoid looking at him. 'I was out of my mind. Ashton had a friend there, another gorgeous hunk. We were snorting cocaine, high as kites. Anyhow, it got to be a threesome. *That's* what he's got on the video.'

'All of it? The cocaine, as well?'

'Yes,' she hissed at him, eyes blazing hatred at having to confess her own sins.

'Are you in the habit of doing coke, Olivia?'

She stamped her foot at his inquisition. 'Everybody does at parties. You know they do,' she shouted at him.

He stared back at her in silent, burning reproof. Many did, but he didn't and she knew it. Apart from alcohol in moderation he never touched recreational drugs and he didn't want to see his sister take the downward spiral that so commonly ended in depression and disaster.

'I didn't do it much until Ashton started getting regular supplies,' she said, trying to mitigate her usage.

Possibly it was true. It would obviously serve Ashton's purpose to get Olivia hooked. 'Okay,' he said calmly. 'I have the picture now. Sit down while I think about how to get you out of this mess.'

Relieved that she had finally loaded it off onto his

shoulders, she dropped onto the sofa and resumed sipping coffee while darting anxious little glances at him.

Jordan mentally plotted the moves that had to be made. Call his lawyer to enquire about all the legal angles. Call his security guy. Olivia would have to be wired and rehearsed into how to get Ashton's blackmail threat on tape. Once he could be threatened with criminal prosecution, Jordan was fairly sure a reasonable settlement could be reached. Pretty-boy Ashton wouldn't enjoy a spell in jail. Olivia had to get stone-cold sober and stay sober until the situation was resolved, and then agree to a month in a rehabilitation centre.

He took out his mobile phone and called his mother. Fortunately she was home and, having been apprised of the problem, agreed to look after Olivia and ensure she was sober for a management meeting tomorrow morning. That gave him the rest of today and tonight with Ivy before he had to act for his sister who certainly deserved to stew overnight for being so damned stupid and careless.

He then called Ray to get the Bentley out to drive Olivia to his mother's Palm Beach residence. He would drive the Porsche there himself in the morning. Having dumped her problem in her brother's hands and now sure he would *fix* it for her, Olivia meekly followed his orders.

Jordan silently determined she would follow a few more in the very near future, like getting her head together enough to make sensible decisions and not take mind-blurring drugs.

It was all so bloody nasty, he thought, as he saw Olivia off in the Bentley. At least taking care of it could wait until tomorrow. Ashton was not about to go anywhere, not until he had milked the golden goose for all he could get.

And Ivy was waiting for him.

Ivy, who'd told him repeatedly she wouldn't fit into his social world: the parties, the gossip, the competitive status thing with its bitchiness and back-biting, the high-flying celebrities who did dabble in cocaine or ecstacy or marijuana for their sensory hits. Part of his mind stood back from it all, like a spectator rather than a participant. But if he took Ivy into it…

No, she didn't fit.

He didn't want her to fit.

It was the difference in her that he found so beguiling.

Somehow he had to keep her out of it, yet keep her in his life.

And his bed.

Determined on making that happen, Jordan headed back into the house, the adrenaline surge of desire kicking in as he went to collect the woman he wanted.

# CHAPTER ELEVEN

Ivy found Margaret surprisingly easy to be with. Aware that the housekeeper had to be curious about the decisions she'd come to in regard to a relationship with Jordan, she'd told her straight out that she owned the rose farm he used for gifts to his girlfriends and hadn't thought the attraction was worth pursuing, given her inside knowledge of his track record with roses.

'Good Heavens! And he kept sending them to your mother!' had been her stunned reaction.

'Yes, it was great for business, but I had to stop it.'

Margaret had burst into laughter, vastly amused by the piquancy of the situation, her eyes twinkling merrily as she'd commented, 'So you're giving him a chance.'

'I do like him.' Not to mention wanting him so intensely it was almost frightening, which the housekeeper probably realised anyway. Ivy couldn't imagine any woman not wanting to experience Jordan Powell in bed. It was his world, not his bed that was the problem.

'Yes, he's very likeable,' Margaret had replied with a fondly indulgent smile. 'I wouldn't work for him if he wasn't.'

This recommendation of Jordan's character from an employee's point of view, added to the masterly way he had handled the scene with his sister, had assured Ivy she wasn't making too big a mistake in getting more involved with him, even if it proved to be a brief affair in the end. Besides, maybe his previous affairs had been littered with fortune-hunters and she wasn't one. That might make some difference.

Margaret had produced a platter of nibbles, suggesting it might tide Ivy over until Jordan had finished with his sister and they could then have lunch together. The brie cheese and dates, little balls of fresh melon wrapped in prosciutto ham, marinated sun-dried tomatoes and olives were all very tempting and without any electric sexual tension knotting her stomach, Ivy suddenly found an appetite.

While picking at the platter, she'd asked Margaret what kind of tours she was interested in since the newspaper was open at the travel section. It turned out that the housekeeper had 'done' most of Europe, saving up all year for an annual trip overseas. The Americas were next on her list, specifically California and Mexico.

'I've never travelled anywhere,' Ivy had confessed. 'Friends of mine were raving about a cruise down the Rhine, and I thought I might try that next year.'

'Why not this year?'

Her heart instantly leapt at Jordan's voice and started banging around her chest as he strode into the kitchen, his face animated with interest. Whatever had transpired with his sister was obviously not lingering in his mind. The blue eyes twinkled with happy speculation as he pursued his point.

'I think they start running those cruises in May. It's only March now. In two months' time, we could be sailing down the Rhine together, Ivy. I'd love to share that part of Europe with you.' He stopped at the island bench, picked a melon ball off the platter, popped it into his mouth, raised his eyebrows at her stunned reaction to his enthusiastic suggestion as he ate the fruit, then asked, 'Can you get away from the farm to do it with me?'

He helped himself to some cheese, slicing up a date to accompany it while Ivy tried to catch her breath. Her mind spun around his extraordinary offer. She could imagine a billionaire on a super-luxury cruise ship like the *Queen Elizabeth II,* or a magnificent chartered yacht, but… 'Is it your kind of thing? I mean…travelling with ordinary tourists?'

'I'll enjoy whatever you enjoy, Ivy.'

Would he really? There was not a hint of doubt in his voice and Ivy could well believe he had schooled himself to be master of any situation. He would probably charm all the other passengers on the ship, make his presence a highlight of their cruise. As for herself, it would be great to have Jordan as her travelling companion, and so much time together would certainly sort out their differences, test how compatible they could be. Make-or-break time for their relationship, she thought.

However, there was one problem he was overlooking. The pipe dream of a marvellous trip together deflated as the reality of her world kicked in. Jordan was undoubtedly accustomed to travelling wherever he wanted whenever he wanted, but…

'We can't do it,' she said with a rueful shake of her head. 'Not this May. You have to book about a year ahead to get on these cruises.'

Determined purpose flashed in his eyes. 'There are always cancellations. Leave it with me and I'll see if I can find us a berth on one.'

He was intent on going and taking her with him. So intent, Ivy suspected he would *buy* a cancellation. It made her feel uncomfortable about it. Why did it matter so much to him? Was he so used to getting his own way nothing was going to stop him? How ruthless was he in wielding his wealth to get what he wanted?

So many questions…and he kept munching away on the hors d'oeuvres as though everything was already settled, his eyes teasing her with the confidence of solving any problem she might still raise. She had succumbed to the power of the man without knowing nearly enough about him, yet the lure of knowing more of him was too strong for her to back off now.

'Okay,' she said slowly. 'I can arrange time off from the farm, but if you do manage to get us on a cruise, Jordan, I insist on paying for my own plane ticket there and back and my share of the tour package.'

No way would she let him think he was *buying* her. Besides, she needed to be independent of him, in case she ended up disliking how it was between them and wanted to walk away.

He grinned, triumphant delight dancing in his eyes. 'Whatever you say, Ivy. I just want us to have this time away together.'

She did, too. It provided a relatively quick proving ground. Not like two years with Ben before finding out he would let her down when she most needed him to be there for her.

'Had enough to eat?' Jordan asked, and her stomach instantly clenched.

No more food.

He wanted sex with her.

'What have you done with your sister?' she asked, sure that he would have already ensured no further interruptions, but curious about the outcome of that meeting.

He grinned and held out his hand to help her off the kitchen stool. 'Sent her home to Mother. Come on. I'll show you the rest of the house. Do you want Margaret to prepare lunch or shall we have an early dinner?'

She took his hand, acutely aware of it enfolding hers as she slid off the stool, wanting to feel him touching her all over, remembering how it had been and eager to experience it again. 'I've had enough to eat for now,' she said, flicking a quick grateful glance at the housekeeper. 'Thank you, Margaret.'

'An early dinner then,' Jordan swiftly instructed.

'Give me a call when you want it,' Margaret drily replied.

Of course she knew what they were about to do, Ivy thought. It was probably a very common scenario with Jordan and she couldn't help wishing it wasn't so. Needing to block out his past and concentrate entirely on the present, her mind snatched at the distraction of his sister and her problems.

'Have you passed the blackmail business over to your mother, too?' she asked as they walked back into the foyer.

'No. I'll deal with it tomorrow when Olivia is sober.' He shot her an apologetic grimace. 'Which means cutting our weekend together short. I'll have to go to Palm Beach in the morning for a family meeting.'

'I hope you can sort something out,' she said sympathetically, thinking it would be horrible to be blackmailed by one's own husband, a man whom Olivia had obviously trusted, however unwisely.

'Don't be concerned about it, Ivy. It will be sorted, one way or another,' he said dismissively. 'In fact, it should be a good lesson for my sister. I intend to make it one, that's for sure,' he added in a tone of determination that would brook no nonsense.

He led her straight to the staircase, no detouring to 'show her the house.' That would come later, after...

Her pulse drummed a faster beat as they mounted the stairs.

'Olivia won't speak to you like that again, either,' he tagged on.

She sighed, relieving the tightness in her chest before slanting an ironic little smile at him. 'I guess all your social set will think the same things about me, Jordan.'

He squeezed her hand hard. 'What *they* think isn't important. Only what *we* have together matters.'

The intensity in his voice sent a quiver of excitement down her spine. She wanted what they could have together, wanted it as much as he did. They reached his bedroom and *nothing* else mattered. They were both insanely lustful, kissing as though there was no tomorrow, removing clothes in urgent haste, falling on the bed in a tangle of legs and arms, reaching for each other, gripping, clinging, caressing with fierce possessiveness, passion pumping through their bodies, fuelling the need to take, to give.

Jordan muttered a curse as he remembered protection, tearing himself away long enough to grab it from a drawer in a bedside table and sheath himself. A weird stab of sadness went through Ivy's heart. No baby with Jordan. That would never happen. It wasn't what this relationship was about. But she had accepted that, hadn't she? And she accepted him now with an intense shaft of pleasure as he came back to her and thrust deeply, driving to the edge of her pulsing womb.

Wild excitement coursed through her with each repeated plunge, the rhythm of it rolling through her in euphoric waves, cresting in marvellous peaks, finally carrying her to an explosion of utter ecstasy and a flood of sweetly lulling peace. *Yes,* she thought blissfully. It was worth any hurt later to have this with Jordan now.

She lay with her head resting over the strong beat of his heart, smiling as she listened to its pace gradually lessen to a quiet, steady thump. *Peace for him, too, after the long waiting,* she thought, and was glad she had surrendered to his patient pursuit. His hands started gliding over the curves of her back and her skin tingled with pleasure. He picked up her plait, removed the rubber band that kept it fastened, and slowly unwound the skeins of her hair, fluffing it out with his fingers when it was freed of its constriction.

'With your hair and skin, you could have posed for Botticelli's *Birth of Venus,*' he murmured. 'It's a wonderful painting, displayed in the Uffizi Gallery in Florence. We could go on to Italy after the cruise and...'

'I don't think so,' Ivy stirred enough to protest. 'We'll be away for a month as it is.' She lifted her head to give him a teasing look. 'And you haven't even shown me all the paintings in this house yet.'

He laughed, raking her hair out on either side of her face. 'You outshine them all, but when I summon up the energy and the inclination I'll give you a tour.'

'Mmmh...I'm not in any hurry.'

'Good, because I don't want to hurry anything this time.'

He kept every kiss and caress deliciously sensual. They moved around each other in a long, languorous dance of gliding, nestling, touching, feeling—a glorious sexual wallowing that simmered with excitement without blazing into imperative need.

He spoke seductively of the fantastic sights they would see and the pleasures they would share in Europe: the amazing array of statues in Prague, the magnificent Schonbrunn Palace in Vienna—'I'll dance you around the gold ballroom'—the vineyards climbing the hills in the Wachau Valley—'We'll go wine-tasting'—the amazing amount of castles along the Rhine, the totally eye-popping quantity of gold decorating the cathedral at the Melk monastery.

'You've seen it all before,' Ivy commented ruefully at one point.

'Not since I was in my teens. My parents took Olivia and me on a world tour as part of our education.'

*Not with another woman then,* Ivy thought with a rush of relief. It was ridiculous wanting something exclusive to herself, knowing how very experienced he was, yet she instantly felt happier in her anticipation of their travels together.

'Besides, I'll enjoy it so much more being with you,' he said, smiling into her eyes, making her heart melt with longing for that to be true.

'Talking of paintings, why did you choose to hang Sydney Nolan's Ned Kelly images in this bedroom?' she asked, wanting to understand more of the man. 'Do you feel some affinity with our famous bushranger or do they simply complement the decor with him wearing his black armour?'

He sidestepped the question, asking, 'Do you like them?'

'They're great, but I thought you'd be more into nudes in here.'

He grinned. 'I don't need that kind of stimulation.'

She laughed, well aware that he had no problem

with impotence. 'You still haven't told me why Ned Kelly?'

His eyes were hooded as his fingertips feathered her lips. 'He reminds me always to be armoured. Especially in the bedroom. Only you have ever made me forget that, Ivy.'

He kissed her, as though wanting to draw that power from her soul, be the man who never lost control again. The simmering excitement instantly escalated, compelling them into another climactic union. It wasn't until long afterwards that Ivy thought about what he'd said about always being armoured.

A billionaire's son, a billionaire in his own right—a target for people who wanted a piece of him for their own ends, in the bedroom and out of it. She imagined very few people would ever fool him in business, but there was a natural vulnerability with intimacy, a wish to trust. Jordan had seen his sister be a victim of it three times because of her wealth.

Was it any wonder that he'd chosen a playboy life-style?

*Essentially a lonely life,* Ivy thought, *always armoured.*

And she was lonely, too.

She enjoyed his company on the tour of his house, enjoyed his company over the delicious dinner Margaret served them, enjoyed the seductively sensual skinny-dipping in the solar-heated pool later in the evening and revelled in the lovemaking that followed. She didn't feel lonely with him and she hoped he didn't feel lonely with her.

Before Jordan had to leave for his family meeting the next morning, they had a happy, relaxed breakfast together and made plans for him to spend the next weekend on the rose farm with her. Ivy drove home feeling brilliantly alive, hoping they could make a lovely self-contained world together that nothing could spoil.

She knew it was a rather silly hope.

Other things would inevitably intrude.

But she was determined to enjoy what she could with Jordan while she could.

# CHAPTER TWELVE

ON Monday, Heather was cock-a-hoop over Ivy's capitulation to a relationship with Jordan Powell, insisting that his persistence proved he was really, really attracted, and the fact that Ivy had enjoyed her time with him showed it to be the right step to take. And when he came to the farm next weekend, could she please, please, please meet him.

Sacha called late in the afternoon to report that no roses had come and what did that mean? Had Ivy met Jordan? Had he persuaded her into seeing more of him? Given an affirmative reply, Sacha was delighted, bubbling over with a list of advantages to be had in associating with such a man, uppermost of which was experiencing a far broader and more civilised way of life than Ivy had been leading on the farm.

Ivy didn't mention the cruise to either woman, thinking it was probably too far in the future to count on, even if Jordan did manage to get them places on it. Who knew what would happen between now and then? She was confident that Heather and Barry could take over running the farm and managing the business on short notice and would be happy to do it for her, if and when required. She simply couldn't shake the fatalistic feeling that this harmony with Jordan was too good to last.

Each night during the week he called her to chat for half an hour or so, just normal conversations about what they'd done throughout the day. Without going into nitty-gritty details, he told her the blackmail threat to his sister had been dealt with, a reasonable divorce settlement agreed upon and Olivia was off to a health spa for some recovery time. And hopefully she would grow some armour against being taken for a ride again.

There was definitely a downside to being incredibly wealthy, Ivy thought. On the other hand, when Jordan arrived at the farm on Friday evening and presented her with confirmation that a stateroom had been secured for them on a cruise in May, she couldn't ignore the suspicion that he'd used the power of wealth to obtain it.

'Did we luck into a cancellation or did you bribe someone to give up their trip, Jordan?' she asked, searching his eyes for the truth, wanting an *honest* answer.

He shrugged. 'I made an offer. Someone took it. What other people choose to do doesn't concern us, Ivy. What matters is we're going.'

It didn't feel right. 'You've spoiled their plans. They would have been looking forward to the cruise. Don't you have any conscience about that?'

He frowned. 'I didn't force their choice. I guess they thought they'd have a lot more spending money for another trip.'

'How much more?'

He waved a dismissive hand. 'It's irrelevant. It's done.'

'But I should pay half of what you paid,' she argued, unable to shake a sense of guilty responsibility.

'No!' He shook his head emphatically. 'I made the decision. I pay the price.'

'We didn't have to go,' she protested, still uncomfortable with how it had been arranged.

'I *want* to.' He scooped her into his embrace, one hand lifting to stroke away her frown as his eyes bored into hers. '*You* want to. Let it be, Ivy.'

Looking at him, feeling him, wanting him, the temptation to let the issue slide pounded through Ivy's mind. *Let it be.* Only a last little niggle made her mutter, 'I wouldn't have minded waiting.'

'This is our time, Ivy,' he murmured seductively, his lips grazing over hers as he added, 'Let's make the most of it.'

*Our time...*

Her heart sank a little at those words, carrying as they did the implication that he expected their time to be limited. By the end of the cruise their relationship would have lasted four months—long enough for Jordan?

But didn't she have the same expectation?

Her body craved what he could give her.

*Make the most of it...*yes.

She couldn't fault Jordan over anything else that weekend. He showed a keen interest in the operation of the rose farm—how it all worked, the standard orders from florists, hotels, big business houses, the more random number of private clients like himself, though he was never to be again, the greenhouses, the packaging room, the refrigerated store of fudges which were supplied by a local woman who'd made an at-home business out of cooking them, the computer system for sales. She enjoyed explaining it all to him.

Graham and Heather came to lunch on Saturday, and Jordan impressed both of them with his appreciation of their contribution to the success of the farm. He didn't present himself as a playboy at all, talking of his own experience with employees, saying how much he valued those he trusted to get the job done. Graham was quickly at ease with him and Heather barely stopped short of drooling—Jordan was so gorgeous!

When the cruise was mentioned, both of them were enthusiastic about a break from the farm for Ivy and assured her they would look after everything.

Ivy let herself relax and enjoy every minute with Jordan. He made it easy, being the perfect lover in every sense.

Again he telephoned her every night during the week, keeping their connection strong. He arrived by helicopter on Saturday morning and flew her to Port Macquarie, a beach resort on the north coast of New South Wales where he was building a new retirement village and nursing home. He shared his vision for it with her, impressing her once again with his caring for the elderly. They ate in the best restaurants the town had to offer and slept in a luxurious apartment that overlooked Flynn's Beach.

He never seemed bored by the weekends he spent on the farm with her, and on his alternate weekends he invariably took Ivy somewhere special—to the Blue Mountains and the amazing Jenolan Caves, to Port Douglas and the Great Barrier Reef, to the Red Centre and Uluru, to the Hunter Valley vineyards. Cost, of course, was no object to Jordan and Ivy decided not to quibble about it. He was taking her on a fantastic ride—the ride of a lifetime—and even if it only lasted six months, which was his uppermost limit for an affair, she was certainly living brilliantly for a while.

More and more she shied away from thinking about the end. Her pleasure in Jordan's company was so intense, the idea of coming to an end was too frightening to contemplate. She loved him, loved everything about him. She lived for the next time they'd be together.

The week before they were due to leave for the cruise, Ivy decided to treat herself to a shopping day, wanting to dress up for the dinners on the ship. Her mother suggested she trawl through the boutiques at Double Bay and meet her for lunch at a bistro she named, since they hadn't seen anything of each other since the gallery exhibition. Having been told of this plan, Jordan invited her to stay overnight with him at Balmoral at the end of the day so she could parade her purchases, which would be fun for both of them.

Ivy was in a happy mood, wandering around the Double Bay shopping centre, looking at the window displays before deciding what might suit her. She was trying on a slinky violet pantsuit in the Liz Davenport boutique, admiring the cut and line of it in the wall mirror, when Olivia Powell walked in with another woman, both of them dressed in high-fashion gear.

Having not met Jordan's sister since the unpleasant scene in his house, she hesitated over whether to acknowledge the brief acquaintance as it would remind Olivia of things she probably wanted to forget. On the other hand, this was the sister of the man she loved. It didn't seem right to ignore her presence.

While Ivy was still dithering over this social dilemma, Olivia glanced around, her gaze picking up Ivy's direct stare at her in the mirror. Her perfectly plucked black eyebrows arched in surprise. Then a look of amusement settled on her face.

'Well, well, if it isn't Jordan's farm girl,' she drawled.

Her companion's attention was instantly drawn to Ivy. 'Who?' she asked.

'Darling, you are looking at the reason why Jordan has been shunning the social scene.'

The other woman goggled at Ivy with avid curiosity. 'A farm girl?'

'Mmmh...so my mother told me when I asked about his new interest.'

'Then what is she doing here?'

'Good question. Maybe he's decided to bring her out of the closet and wants her decently clothed.'

There was no attempt to lower their voices. Ivy heard every word and the unfriendliness of Olivia's attitude, the scorn in her tone, made her stomach churn with a sense of sick vulnerability. Jordan wasn't here to fend off his sister's nastiness and Ivy knew, even before Olivia started strolling towards her, knew from the malicious glint in her eyes, that she was about to be subjected to a humiliating public attack.

Pride made her stand her ground.

Olivia closed in, her mouth curling with a savage mockery. 'Did you stick Jordan for a dress allowance, Ivy?'

Embarrassment was burning her cheeks. Her mouth was dry. She quickly worked some moisture into it, lifted her chin, and answered. 'No. I've taken no money from Jordan at all, Olivia.'

'Oh? Investing in yourself, are you? Showing him if you can look the part, you might get further than his bedroom?'

Ivy shook her head, finding it difficult to counter such virulence. 'Why are you gunning for me like this, Olivia?' she blurted out. 'I've never done anything bad to you.'

'Your kind has taken too many bites out of me. No doubt you're as sweet as pie to Jordan, just as Ashton was to me, but let me tell you, my brother is the clever one. You're wasting your time and your money on him. You can crawl into his bed, but you won't get past his head which is screwed on very tightly. Put one foot over the boundaries he's set and you'll get dumped, just like all the rest.'

Boundaries…keeping her in his closet…no social contact with *his* friends…the realisation that Olivia was telling exactly how it was hit into Ivy's heart like a sledgehammer. She couldn't protest. It was pointless even carrying on a conversation. She looked into Olivia's blue eyes—Jordan's eyes—and knew what she had known all along but this time much more painfully. She was not of their world, never would be.

'Thank you,' she said. 'I appreciate your caring.'

At least Olivia's startled look at her response was some balm to her pride.

'Please excuse me,' she went on with as much dignity as she could muster. 'I need to change back into my own clothes. Rest assured I'll be out of your brother's life very soon.'

She didn't wait for a reply, heading straight for the change room, no longer interested in buying stylish clothes. Thankfully Olivia and her companion were gone when she emerged. Not wanting to run into them again and grateful that the bistro Sacha had named was in a back street, she hurried there, sitting over a cup of coffee while she waited for her mother, silently berating herself for falling in love with a man who should have always remained a fantasy.

Sacha arrived, beaming pleasure in this outing together until she saw there were no shopping bags at Ivy's feet. 'You haven't found *anything* you like?' she wailed in disappointment.

Ivy managed an ironic smile. 'I met Jordan's sister and lost the plot.'

Her mother frowned and sat down. 'What do you mean?'

'I mean I realised how big a fool I was for falling in love with him and I should end it right now.'

Sacha gaped at her in horror. 'But, darling, you're going on this marvellous cruise with him next week.'

She couldn't, not feeling so torn up inside. Tears welled into her eyes. She hadn't cried since her father's death, but this was like a death, too, the killing of hopes and dreams she should never have let into her heart. Embarrassed at breaking down, she covered her face with her hands and tried desperately to choke off the heaving sensation making her chest unbearably tight.

'Oh, Ivy!'

She barely heard the anguished cry from her mother, but she felt the warm hug around her shoulders and the stroking of her hair. The caring gestures made it more difficult to bring herself under control but she finally managed it, hating the thought of making a spectacle of herself in a public place.

'I'm okay,' she bit out. 'Sorry. Please…do sit down again.'

'Ivy, I know I haven't been the kind of mother you probably wanted but…let me help.'

'There's nothing to help. It was a mistake.'

Sacha resumed her seat on the other side of the table as Ivy blotted her face with a hastily grabbed tissue from her handbag. Aware that her mother was viewing her with anxious concern, she took several deep, calming breaths and forced a rueful little smile.

'I should have kept my head. That's all,' she said with cutting finality.

'Love isn't about keeping one's head,' Sacha said wryly. 'It wasn't sensible for your father and I to fall in love with each other—a hippie artist and a Vietnam veteran who needed a colourful butterfly to give him some zest for life again. It was even less sensible for us to get married, but you know, Ivy, I've never regretted it. Robert was the only man I've ever loved and I'm glad I had that experience.'

Ivy sighed, remembering how she'd argued herself into the affair with Jordan...as an experience worth having. 'I guess the difference is...Dad loved you back.'

'Are you sure Jordan doesn't love you?' Sacha queried. 'He has been very, very attentive to pleasing you.'

'More in lust with me than loving me, I'd say.'

'Love and lust can be intertwined.'

Ivy shrugged. 'On his weekends at the farm we went to a couple of dinner parties at my friends' homes. They wanted to meet him and he was always a charming guest.' She looked bleakly at her mother. 'On my weekends with him, we always went away somewhere. I've never been introduced to any of his friends. Only to his sister by accident. What does that tell you?'

'Maybe that he wanted you to himself.'

'That's not what Olivia thinks. Fit for the bedroom but not for being a partner in any public sense.'

'What she thinks does not make her an authority on what her brother feels,' Sacha retorted with an odd look of determination. 'You should confront him directly about this, Ivy. All those roses he sent me...he wanted a chance with you. At least give him the chance to explain how *he* sees your relationship.'

Ivy remembered Jordan's insistence on her being fair,

not making assumptions about him, despite all the evidence that painted a very clear picture.

He hadn't actually let her down.

She had let herself be blinded by her growing love for him, wanting what was special between them to encompass much more than it did. Nevertheless, her mother was right. It was only fair to tell Jordan face to face why she had decided their time was over.

'Don't worry. He won't be sending you any more roses,' she said dryly. 'He's expecting me at Balmoral this afternoon. I'll go and see him, speak to him.'

'Make sure you listen, too, Ivy,' Sacha advised, still looking as though she wanted to argue Jordan's case.

*Because of who he is,* Ivy thought. The billionaire tag *was* blinding and the power of wealth was seductive, providing all the luxurious living she had done over the past two months, which she had undeniably enjoyed.

Because she had been with him.

Weaving foolish dreams.

'I'll listen,' she promised, picking up the menu from its stand on the table. 'I don't want to talk about this any more, Sacha. Let's order lunch.'

She had no appetite.

Her stomach was cramped with tension.

She simply wanted some distraction from what she had to do later in the afternoon. They could talk about her mother's paintings—the life she had made for herself apart from her marriage. It was what she had to do without Jordan—make a life alone because there would be no other man. There couldn't be another man like him. It just wasn't possible.

# CHAPTER THIRTEEN

HIS mobile telephone rang just as Jordan was about to go into a meeting with a consortium of property developers. *Ivy,* he thought, smiling as he whipped the phone out of the breast pocket of his suit. It was almost three o'clock. Possibly she had finished shopping and was about to drive over to Balmoral. No doubt she'd chat with Margaret until he arrived. He motioned for his aide-de-camp to go ahead and settle everyone in the boardroom as he answered the call.

'Jordan, it's Olivia.'

A frown replaced the smile. What did his sister want of him now?

'I think I might have made a mistake,' she went on.

He rolled his eyes. Indulging his sister by listening to her troubles was not on at the moment. 'Olivia, I have people waiting on me for a business meeting,' he said curtly. 'I'll call you back when it's over.'

'No, wait!' Urgent anxiety was in her voice. 'It's about Ivy.'

His impatience was instantly ejected by red alert signals going off in his brain. The only time Olivia had met Ivy she had been extremely nasty to her. 'What mistake did you make?' he asked, needing to know the worst.

'I was with Caroline Sheldon and we went to Double Bay to do some shopping.'

Tension whipped through Jordan's body at the mention of Double Bay and Caroline Sheldon, who could be as bitchy as Olivia about other women. This was shaping up to be a bad scene.

'Anyhow, we walked into the Liz Davenport boutique and there was Ivy, trying on a pantsuit I know was priced at over seven hundred dollars.'

'So?' he snapped.

'Well, naturally I thought you'd given her the money to make herself look fashionable enough to fit into our crowd. I did the same thing with Ashton.'

'Ivy is nothing like Ashton,' he grated out, furious with Olivia's assumption.

'How was I supposed to know that? You've kept her to yourself all this time. Mum told me she worked on a farm and that fitted what I saw of her with you.'

'Ivy *owns* a very profitable rose farm. It's a solid business. I've checked it out,' he almost shouted in his chagrin. 'She can afford to buy whatever clothes she likes.'

'Well, it's your fault for keeping so mum about her,' came the typical defence. Everything was always someone's else's fault in his sister's life.

He sliced straight to the vital point. 'What did you do, Olivia?'

She huffed. 'I've had to ask you to rescue me. I liked the idea of saving you for once.'

'Saving me from what?'

'A fortune-hunter! Except...I don't think she is one. What she said back to me...the way she looked...it didn't fit at all. And the more I thought about it, the more I felt I should 'fess up to you about making a mistake, because I think she means to walk out of your life and you might not want her to.'

'You're quite right. I don't,' he said grimly, knowing he could very well lose Ivy because of Olivia's interference.

'At least give me credit for telling you, Jordan. I'm sure you can fix it up now that you know.'

Removing all guilt from herself.

Jordan unclenched his jaw enough to say, 'Thank you, Olivia. You might also call Caroline Sheldon and correct the false impression you gave her of Ivy who happens to be the most genuine and delightful person I've ever met.'

It was the truth. Not once had she ever given him reason to doubt the character she had shown him throughout the whole time they had spent together.

'Then why haven't you introduced her around?' came the swift retort, loaded with self-justification.

'Because I'm still in the process of winning her over to wanting to be in my life.'

'Why wouldn't she want to?'

Unimaginable to Olivia.

'Because she doesn't feel she belongs with people like you,' he answered harshly, unable to contain his anger. 'And you know what, Olivia? She doesn't!'

He pressed the disconnect button and stood still for several moments, needing to calm himself and assess the situation. His heart was thumping like a battle-drum. What the hell could he do to counter what Olivia had done! Some things couldn't be fixed. Ivy would be all the more convinced now that she wouldn't fit into his world. That conviction had taken her away from him once. He had to fight it again to keep her.

Ivy had brought more joy into his life than any other

woman. It was always a pleasure to be with her, in bed and out of it. He'd had more fun at her friends' parties—relatively uncomplicated people, satisfied with their lives in the country—than he did at the parties revolving around who's who with the socialite A-list. He knew where she was coming from, knew what she would go back to and, although he understood why, somehow he had to stop it because he was not prepared to accept the hole she would leave in his life.

He quickly tapped in her mobile number, needing communication.

No answer.

She'd turned it off.

Was she on her way home?

No, he decided. Ivy would not skip out on him as she had before. There'd been too much between them to go without a word. She'd promised to be fair, which surely meant facing him with whatever Olivia had said. Therefore, she would be at Balmoral later this afternoon, as arranged. He would have the chance then to employ every hold he could think of to sway her into staying with him. Whatever it took, he was not going to lose her.

Feeling more confident he could do it, one way or another, Jordan switched his mind to the business meeting, determined to get through it as fast as possible. Two frustrating hours later he was out of it, trying to call Ivy again. No answer. He called Margaret, needing to know if Ivy had arrived.

'Yes. About twenty minutes ago. But…' She left the word hanging, as though in two minds whether to express the thought.

'But what?' Jordan pressed, wanting every bit of information he could get about the situation. Forewarned, forearmed.

'Not that it's any of my business...'

'Make it your business, Margaret.'

'Well, she's not herself. You know how much I like Ivy and we always have a nice chat. She's never been uppity or off-putting like some I could mention. I actually look forward to her visits because she's so nice and natural and funny, and I'm quite sure she enjoys my company, too. But not today. I think something's upset her. Badly. She declined a cup of coffee and said she'd wait for you out in the pagoda.'

Not in his house. Withdrawing...

'She didn't bring in an overnight bag, either,' Margaret went on worriedly. 'I checked.'

No intention to stay.

'And if she'd been happily shopping, which you told me was the plan, I'm sure she would have been all bubbly about what she'd bought. So, since you've asked my opinion, I think something's very wrong, Jordan, and I don't like it.'

Neither did he.

'Her phone is switched off. Would you please take your receiver down to the pagoda so I can speak to her?'

'Okay. Doing it now.'

His whole body was tight with tension as he waited, his mind zapping through an array of opening lines, wanting what might be the most effective one.

'Hello...' Her voice was dull, no joy in it.

'Ivy, Olivia called me,' he rushed out. 'She's very sorry for what she said to you.'

Silence.

Then flatly, 'I'd rather not discuss it on the phone,

Jordan. We'll talk when you get home. Thank you, Margaret.'

Cut off.

But at least she was waiting for him.

Peak-hour traffic slowed his journey to a crawl. Jordan applied several relaxation techniques to keep tension at bay. Nothing worked. At one of the many red lights delaying his progress, he removed his suit coat and tie, flicked open the top buttons of his shirt and thought about how to get Ivy naked. Bodies spoke a better language than words. The sex between them was still fantastic. She couldn't deny that.

But it hadn't stopped her from walking away in the past.

He clamped down on the negative thought. He'd win her over. He'd done it before. He'd do it again. That determination rode with him the rest of the way home.

Margaret intercepted him as he strode through the house to the back terraces. She handed him a tray which held a wine bottle in an ice-bucket, two glasses and a selection of savoury dips and crackers. 'This might help,' she said.

'Thanks, Margaret.' He took the tray. 'Ivy still out there?'

'Hasn't returned to the house,' she threw over her shoulder as she moved quickly to open the exit door for him.

'It's Olivia's doing,' he tossed at her as he passed, too vexed with the situation to accept the blame shooting at him from his housekeeper's eyes. Damn it all! He'd done the best he could, keeping Ivy away from the gossip-mill of the socialite world, the jealous snipes, the boozy parties, the self-destructive fools who indulged in recreational drugs. He shouldn't be shot down over his sister's transgression.

A wave of anger crashed through him.

There was so much good to be had in his world. Hadn't he shown Ivy that side of it? And he could keep on showing her if she'd just let him. Ending it here and now wasn't fair. He'd make her see that. Make her *feel* it!

Ivy had her gaze trained on the brilliant view of Sydney Harbour from her cushioned seat in the pagoda, but the images of boats and white-crested blue water barely impinged on her consciousness. Waiting for Jordan was like being in a suspended state of animation, knowing she couldn't go back to what they'd had together, yet unable to move forward until after she had laid that out to him.

In a way it was a relief that Olivia had told him about their encounter. At least she wouldn't have to explain that scene. Whether his sister was sorry or not didn't matter. It was best to end the relationship anyway.

Footsteps clacking down the path from the pool terrace, fast and purposeful.

It had to be Jordan.

Ivy tensed, feeling the power of the man coming closer and closer. He stepped into the pagoda, carrying a tray of refreshments and a ruthless air of command that instantly sent tingles of alarm down Ivy's spine. There would be no gracious letting go. Jordan was intent on fighting for what he wanted and exploiting every bit of vulnerability he could use.

As he had before, she reminded herself.

Except she wouldn't fall for it this time.

Her mind was steel on that point, even though her body quivered weakly at his nearness.

'A glass of wine?' he asked, setting the tray on the table, laser-blue eyes searching hers for some chink of giving.

'No, thank you. I'll be driving home very shortly, Jordan. I was thinking…maybe you could contact the people you bought the cruise package from and give it back to them. I won't be going and if you don't want to go without me, it will be wasted.'

He left the table, took a seat on the cushioned bench facing hers, and leaned forward, elbows on his knees, transmitting a patience that had a belligerent edge to it. 'What's behind this decision, Ivy?' he shot at her.

'Our time is up,' she answered with direct simplicity

He shook his head. 'That's not true. What did Olivia say to make you think that?'

'She made me see what I am to you.'

'Olivia doesn't have a clue what you are to me,' was his emphatic retort. 'She only sees things through her own eyes.'

'No. It rang all the bells. You have been a great lover, Jordan, and I thank you for all the pleasure you've given me. I wish I could have been more to you than your closet mistress, but…'

'My *what?*'

Ivy's heart kicked into a gallop at the violence of feeling exploding from his mouth, zapping from his eyes, shooting him to his feet in furious outrage, his hands clenched. She'd never seen Jordan angry and it was frightening.

'Please…will you sit down and hear me out?' she

quickly begged, scared that he might use physical force to bring her back to him.

'You're talking garbage, Ivy.'

'No, I'm not.'

He glared his impatience with her denial, saw the determined jut of her chin, the rejection of what he might do in her eyes, and resumed his seat, stretching his arms out along the backrest to defuse any sense of threat, watching her with an intensity that shredded Ivy's nerves. One hand flipped a dismissal as he said, 'It hasn't been an easy three hours since Olivia's call to me. I would have corrected what she said to you a lot sooner if you'd contacted me. Whatever you're thinking now is wrong, Ivy.'

'Then why have you never introduced me to your friends, your social circle?' she bored in.

'Because you claimed, right from the start, that you wouldn't fit into my scene, and I wanted the pleasure of your company without anything negative taking you away from me.'

The calm, matter-of-fact reply confused Ivy for a few moments. She *had* used their different worlds as a point of resistance to Jordan, but he had proved he could fit into hers. He hadn't given her the chance to come to terms with his. And hadn't planned to. Ever. He had set out to keep her happy in his bed because that was where he wanted her. There'd been no intention to see if she could be his partner in life.

'That's not how a real relationship works,' she said with conviction. 'You have been keeping me in your closet, Jordan, distracting me from that truth by taking me on a lot of marvellous out-of-the-way rides.'

'Wouldn't you say we got to know each other very well on those rides? And enjoyed being together?'

'Of course, I enjoyed it. Who wouldn't? You swept me off my feet in every sense, made a perfect fantasy of our time together. And you would have kept doing it with the cruise, as well, and I would have been too besotted with you to notice.'

'Notice what?'

'How it was simply getaway time for you. Not real time. And when the pleasure of it finally wore thin, I'd be jettisoned from your life, like all the rest.' She gave him a bleak little smile. 'Without the roses.'

He stared at her in silence.

No quick comeback.

No rebuttal.

She remembered the emphasis he'd placed on honesty and realised he couldn't lie to her.

The hope for some different outcome died in her heart.

He didn't love her as she loved him.

Their time was up and there was no point in any more talking, no point in staying another minute. She felt totally spent. It was an act of will to pick up her handbag and rise to her feet. A spurt of tears blurred her eyes as she looked at Jordan for the last time. She had to force herself to say the final words.

'Goodbye. Don't come after me, Jordan. It's over.'

# CHAPTER FOURTEEN

'No!'

The shock of absolute finality from Ivy catapulted Jordan from the bench, the need to bar her exit from the pagoda slicing straight through the conflicts raging in his mind.

He couldn't let her go.

That was the bottom line.

He stood in her way, hands held up in a commanding appeal to stop. She did, actually reeling back a step to keep distance between them, clutching her handbag as a defensive shield, her lovely green eyes awash with tears, drowning pools of despair begging him to let her pass without interference.

It screwed up his thoughts and emotions even further. He cared about this woman, didn't want to give her pain, hated her distress. The urge to sweep her into his embrace and give her every physical comfort he could— kiss her tears away, cradle her head on his shoulder, stroke her hair—stormed through him. Only the absolute certainty in the saner part of his mind that it would be a mistake held him back. She would fight him, hate him for not respecting her decision.

He had to fight the decision, change it around. But what with? She had spoken the truth. All the weekends with Ivy *had* been a getaway from his normal life. It had made them special. *She* had made them special. He hadn't wanted anything she might not like to intrude on what they had together.

He'd deliberately spun that strategy out, using the cruise to keep it going, because he had expected their relationship to hit a snag somewhere along the line and come to an end. It was a perfectly rational expectation. He had actually anticipated his *real life* becoming one of the snags, not the omission of it.

'I simply wanted you to be happy with me, Ivy,' he explained. 'Happy with where we were and what we were doing.'

'Happy to be in your bed,' she retorted fiercely, dashing the tears from her eyes, her chest heaving as she scooped in a deep breath and faced him with what she believed. 'It's just sex with you, isn't it, Jordan? You're not looking for a life partner. You certainly don't see me as one. So why don't you *simply* admit that and let me pass because we are not going anywhere any more.'

A life partner...

No, he hadn't been looking for one, had been determined on not going down the marital road with all its pitfalls to suck a man down. Yet, might they not be avoided with a woman like Ivy?

Why not try it?

The thought zapped into Jordan's mind and grew powerfully persuasive tentacles. Margaret approved of her. Having the two women in his household sharing an easy bond was a very positive plus. Besides, a marriage proposal was the strongest possible way of rebutting the reasons Ivy gave for walking away.

It proved he wanted a real relationship with her. He wouldn't lose her today. That was certain. As for the future, if it didn't work out, Ivy was not the kind of person who would milk him for all she could get. He was as sure of that as it was possible to be. Besides, right now he didn't care if there was a price to be paid down the line. He wasn't ready to let her go.

A public engagement would make the transition to sharing his world much easier. People would be currying favour from her, not wanting to upset her in any fashion. It gave her protection from the gossips, from the guys who might want to hit on her, and the mean-spirited women who might be jealous of her success with him.

Most critically, it bought more time.

'You're wrong, Ivy,' he said, his conviction that this was the right move already cemented in his mind. 'I was keeping you to myself because what we have together was and is the most important thing in my life and I want it to go on being the most important. I hadn't planned to ask you at this point but I will because I believe we do and can have a great relationship, regardless of our different worlds.'

He saw the outright rejection of him begin to waver in her eyes, felt an exhilarating burst of adrenaline at the sure prospect of winning. *Seal the deal,* he told himself. Then he could take her in his arms and make her happy with him again.

'Ask me what?' Even her voice was furred with uncertainty.

'To marry me.'

She looked totally stunned.

He spread his hands in open appeal as he nailed home what he was offering. 'To become my wife, Ivy. To be my partner in life. To share everything, the good and the bad.'

He took a step towards her.

She didn't move. Her eyes were glazed with shock.

'To make a future together, have children,' he went on, surprising himself with what was coming out of his mouth, but not caring, intent on pursuing the need to have this woman, moving closer, reaching out, curling his hands around her upper arms, his eyes boring a determined hole through her shock, to engage her mind, her heart with a completely different scenario to the one she had brought to him today.

'Ivy, you're the right woman for me,' he pressed. 'Don't you see that? Don't you *feel* it?'

She stared at him, her gaze swallowed up by deep green pools of vulnerability. He saw her struggling with the wish to believe. There was no resistant strength in her hands when he took her handbag and tossed it onto the bench, no resistance in her body as he drew it against his. He gently cupped her face, the fire in his belly blazing from his eyes.

'I won't ask you to give up your farm. I won't demand that you do anything you don't want to do. We'll sort out how best to work our partnership as we go along, find a balance that we're both comfortable with. We've been good at that so far, haven't we?'

She was listening, still wary of believing but weighing up what he was saying, wanting it to be true.

He had to make it ring true.

'And if you're ready and willing to mix in with my usual social scene, we can start that this weekend,' he went on, driven to rid her of all doubt. 'I haven't been hiding you in my closet, Ivy. I've been waiting for you to feel confident at my side, confident enough to take on anything with me because I'm your man. Not a playboy. Your man,' he repeated emphatically.

Tears welled into her eyes again, but there was hope

shining through them, hope and something that twisted Jordan's heart, making him want to wrap her tightly in his arms and hold her safe from the whole world and any hurt in it.

She lifted her arms and wound them around his neck. Her lips quivered invitingly. The tension inside him eased. He had won. She wanted him to kiss her and he did with a passion, determined on making her feel she was the right woman for him, the only woman. And the way she kissed him back made him feel it, too. Excitement sizzled through him, urging him to go further, take all he could of her, complete possession.

No. Better not to risk it. Not when she'd thought he only wanted her for sex. There had to be some talking first. Her body had always responded to him, but he had to be sure her mind was clear of all bad thoughts, clear on where they were now heading. She hadn't agreed to it yet. Not verbally. Though one thing was certain. She was not about to leave him now.

He forced himself to check the desire that could so swiftly consume good intentions and slowly managed to control himself enough to murmur against her lips, 'Say yes, Ivy. Say yes to us having a future together.'

'Yes,' she said on a sigh of surrender that was blissfully sweet to his ears.

She lifted her head back and gave him a tremulous smile. 'I'm sorry I got it so wrong, Jordan.'

'Not your fault.' He stroked the lovely tilted corner of her mouth. 'I did straighten Olivia out on how I felt about you. What we'll do now is make it very public so there'll be no mistake from anyone about where our relationship stands.'

'Public?' Heat rushed into her cheeks at the thought of being thrust into the kind of limelight that had never shone on her life. 'Jordan, are you sure about this? Maybe we should wait awhile.'

He shook his head. 'Yes means yes, Ivy.' He wanted to get her tied to him as irrevocably as he could at this point. If either of them had doubts about marriage later, they could back out of it then. 'You planned on staying here tonight. Before you go home in the morning, I'll take you shopping for an engagement ring.' He grinned. 'What would you like? A diamond? An emerald to match your eyes? A ruby? Sapphire?'

She burst into nervous laughter. 'I haven't thought about it, Jordan. This is so...so...not what I expected from you.'

'You can look at the ring on your finger and know it's real. What's more, I'll have an announcement of our engagement put in Saturday's *Morning Herald* so everyone will know it's real. And an engagement party. I'll ask my mother to put one on.'

Plans were racing through his mind. He'd sweep Ivy along with him so fast, she wouldn't have time to have second thoughts; he'd open the closet door with a vengeance, plunge her into the society circus with his ring to make her sparkle at his side, then straight off on the cruise where he could keep reminding her of how good they were together. No negative comeback from that course of action.

'It will have to be this Saturday night because we leave for our cruise next Wednesday.'

She looked dazzled. 'What has to be this Saturday night?'

'Our engagement party. Come on, Ivy...' He dropped his embrace to take her hand and draw her with him. 'Let's go up to the house and break the news to Margaret.

Ask her to cook us a celebration dinner. Call my mother. Call your mother.'

He grabbed her handbag and passed it to her, then saw the tray he'd set on the table. 'Better take that with us. We can swap the bottle of wine for champagne. This is definitely the night for it.'

Champagne… Ivy felt as though she had imbibed a whole bottle of it already. Her head was fizzing from the sheer rush of Jordan's proposals…marriage, children, introduction to his family and friends…all unimaginable an hour ago. He had suddenly presented her with a dream life and it didn't feel quite real. Maybe they could make it real. Certainly he was brimming over with confidence, pouring out his vision of their future together as they walked up to the house.

The weird part was she had been about to walk out of his life because he had avoided making a public show of their relationship, and now she felt frightened of what that show might entail. Jordan was probably the most eligible bachelor in Australia. Another girlfriend was not big news, but the notorious billionaire playboy getting married would instantly beam a spotlight on the fiancée whom no one knew anything about. How was she going to handle it? This was a huge leap from her normal, quiet life.

She tried to calm her wildly skittering heart by telling herself Jordan would be at her side. He was used to handling everything, master of any situation. And being with the man she loved…wasn't that what she most wanted? Nothing else should really matter.

It suddenly struck her that Jordan hadn't spoken of loving her.

But he must.

Why ask her to marry him if he didn't?

Besides, she hadn't said it, either.

It didn't really need to be put into words.

She followed him into the kitchen where he set the tray on the island bench and whipped the bottle of wine out of the ice bucket, brandishing it at Margaret who looked relieved to see them together. 'This is not good enough for us tonight,' he said with a happy grin. 'Congratulations are in order, Margaret. Ivy has just agreed to marry me.'

Her mouth dropped open in surprise. She goggled at Jordan for a moment, then looked at Ivy as though wondering if she'd heard right.

'It's true,' Ivy said with a wry little smile, thinking they were probably going to get this reaction from everyone. After all, she hadn't expected it herself.

'Oh!' Margaret cried, suddenly clapping her hands in delight. 'You've made a wonderful choice, Jordan! You're the best, Ivy. The very best.'

'Glad to have your approval,' Jordan rolled out, clearly riding a high. 'You have an hour to whip us up a splendid dinner. I'll take this tray of titbits, minus the wine, into the lounge room and get a bottle of champagne from the bar there. Ivy and I have some calls to make.'

Margaret ignored him, walking over to Ivy, taking her hands and pressing them with pleasure. 'I'll do everything I can to see that you're happy here, my dear.'

The kind acceptance and welcome from Jordan's housekeeper brought a lump of emotional gratitude to Ivy's throat. She could only manage a husky, 'Thank you.'

'Go on now. You'll be fine,' Margaret assured her.

The housekeeper's confidence in her settled some of Ivy's nerves, but the sense of being on a roller-coaster ride persisted, especially as she listened to Jordan's side of his conversation with his mother.

He'd poured them glasses of champagne, made a toast to a happy future together, saw her seated on a sofa, and was walking around the room as he talked, giving out a crackling energy that was not about to be dampened by anything.

'Mum, I need you to do me a favour. I've just asked Ivy Thornton to marry me. She's said yes. And I want you to throw us an engagement party this coming Saturday night.'

His vivid blue eyes sparkled wickedly as he listened to what was undoubtedly a tirade of disbelief at the other end of the line. 'Mum, I'm thirty-six years old and in full possession of all my faculties. I do not need your stamp of approval on my bride-to-be.' He grinned at Ivy. 'I love everything about her, and you will, too. That's all you have to know.'

*Love...*

Her love for him poured into a smile that beamed with happiness. It was okay to marry him. As long as they loved each other, they could make it work.

'No, I don't want to wait. We're buying the ring tomorrow and we're flying off to Europe next week. I know it's short notice but I'm sure you and your personal assistant can make it happen. Get Olivia to help with the guest list. She owes me big-time.'

He grimaced at whatever his mother said next. Then his face set in a look of ruthless determination. 'No. No meeting beforehand. I won't have Ivy subjected to any uneasiness caused by you or Olivia, who did her worst today. We'll turn up on Saturday night and I expect both of you to be very warm and welcoming. As you should be.'

It was strange seeing this formidable side of him—the

exercise of unrelenting power—though she had glimpsed it before when Olivia had turned up with her blackmail problem. This was how he dealt with his world, she realised, the other side of the charm he had brought into her world.

She needed to know a lot more about Jordan's life. Her instincts said he was the right man for her, but experiencing a *real* relationship with him would definitely make her feel more confident that a marriage between them could work. However, what she needed most was for this current sense of *un*reality to leave her.

'All set,' he said with satisfaction, having ended the call. 'Would you like to contact your mother now? Tell her the news and invite her to the party?'

'Yes, I will.'

Sacha's reaction would surely lift her spirits, generate the excitement that Jordan's proposal should be generating. She fossicked in her handbag for her mobile telephone, found it, switched it on, took a deep breath and set about correcting the false impression of Jordan she'd given her mother earlier today.

Sacha was ecstatic at the marvellous turnaround from break-up to marriage, babbling on about being right about the roses and how happy she was for Ivy. Of course she would attend the engagement party. With bells on! She finished up with, 'I've always wanted the best for you, darling, and I'm sure with Jordan, you'll have it.'

It left a more relaxed smile on Ivy's face as she put her phone away. Margaret had said she was *the best* for him. Her mother thought Jordan was *the best* for her. She remembered at their meeting in the Queen Victoria Building, when Jordan had been pushing for a relationship, he'd argued, *It might be the best thing either of us could ever have.*

All she had to do was believe it.

Jordan took her hands and drew her up from the sofa, a teasing twinkle in his eyes. 'Happy now?'

Her heart swelled with love for him. She wound her arms around his neck, her eyes sparkling with the wonder of what had happened between them. 'Very happy,' she answered.

He kissed her forehead and murmured, 'No more bad thoughts. We're good together, Ivy, and everyone is going to see that. We'll show them.'

'Yes,' she said. It was true. They were good together.

And her whole body pulsed happily with that truth as he fitted it to his and kissed her with more than enough fervour to drive it home. An exultant joy danced through her mind. This was her man. Regardless of what the future held for them, she was never going to regret having him.

# CHAPTER FIFTEEN

THE first clash over Jordan's world came at the jeweller's when they were looking at a fabulous array of rings. Ivy had never seen such beautifully cut and crafted gemstones. They were light years above the usual diamond engagement rings one saw in shop windows. She was so dazzled by them, she looked at Jordan in disbelief when he asked her to choose what most appealed to her. They were simply beyond anything she had imagined and her mind cringed at what any one of them might cost.

'You choose,' she pleaded, realising he was intent on having her wear a ring that reflected his buying power and gave her instant status as his fiancée.

Without the slightest hesitation he reached for a brilliant square-cut emerald mounted in the centre of two rows of diamonds, the first row square cut like the emerald, the second shaped like tear drops. 'Let's try this one,' he said, smiling as he took her left hand and slid it on her third finger. 'Perfect fit, too. Do you like it?'

'It's…it's magnificent, Jordan.' What else could she say?

'Great! We'll take it,' he said with satisfaction.

'A fine choice!' the jeweller approved. 'May I show you the accompanying pieces, sir? A matching diamond and emerald necklace and earrings.' He smiled

at Ivy. 'I'm sure they would look splendid on Miss
Thornton.'

She was speechless, appalled at the suggestion.

'Please do,' Jordan said, obviously enthused by the
idea.

The jeweller swiftly removed himself to some back
room to fetch them and Ivy seized the chance for a private protest. 'You mustn't buy them for me, Jordan,'
she cried anxiously. 'The ring is enough. More than
enough.'

He smiled indulgently at her. 'Ivy, I can afford to
spoil you with some fine jewellery. And if it does look
splendid on you, we'll go shopping for a suitable dress
to show it off at our engagement party.'

'No!' She shook her head vehemently. 'They'll all
know you bought it. They'll think...' Just like his sister
did, that he was fitting her out to be introduced to his
social scene—Cinderella striking it rich. 'I don't want it,
Jordan,' she said with a fierce surge of pride. 'I'll dress
myself and if I'm not good enough for you as I am...'

'Hey, hey!' he cut in, frowning at her reaction to his
plan. 'I only meant to give you the pleasure of outshin-
ing everyone on the night.'

She glared at him. 'I'm not a trophy woman, remember? It's not me.' She looked down at the ring on her finger, beginning to feel uncomfortable about that, too.

He put his hand over it to prevent her from taking
it off. 'You're going to be my wife, Ivy. This ring is
part and parcel of that position. I want you to have it.
Okay?'

He spoke with soft persuasion but there was inflexible
purpose in his eyes, demanding that she surrender to his
will on this issue. She heaved a sigh to ease the tightness
in her chest and nodded. 'Okay to the ring. But not to

you buying me anything else.' She was absolutely inflexible herself on that point. The memory of yesterday's encounter in the Double Bay boutique was too fresh to forget. No way would she invite rotten assumptions to be made about her.

He raised his hand to gently stroke her cheek, which was burning with the ferocity of her feeling. 'You're more than good enough for me and I hope you never change,' he said with what looked like genuine appreciation in his eyes. 'Wear whatever you like on Saturday night, as long as you also wear this ring because it says what I feel about you for the whole world to see.'

Her pride splintered into a quick apology. 'Sorry for being so prickly.' Her eyes pleaded for understanding. 'I guess it's a lot to take in all at once. I won't let you down at the party. I *can* look presentable, you know.'

'Don't let it be too important, Ivy. It's not,' he assured her.

But somehow it was. She was about to be publicly linked with Jordan Powell, and she needed to look like a match for him, not feel out of place at his side. After the purchase of the ring had been made, she delayed her return to the farm, driving over to Double Bay and not leaving until she was satisfied that her wardrobe had been suitably replenished with clothes which would not raise a critical eyebrow anywhere.

The sheer extravagance of what she'd bought nagged at her on the drive home. She was not used to spending so much money on herself. There'd only been the one wild spree for Sacha's exhibition, motivated mostly to avoid criticism, which was what she was doing again now. Jordan was right. She shouldn't let what others might think become too important, nor should she let her pride prevent him from giving her whatever he wanted to give her. If it gave him pleasure to adorn her like a queen, she should accept it gracefully, especially when she was his wife.

She wanted to fit into his world. For him. She needed to learn how to do it, not buck at every entry point. It was important to be more open-minded now, adapt to whatever company she was in. He'd done it for her. Loving him, having his love…keeping that at the heart of everything would surely smooth the path to the future they wanted together.

It was almost four o'clock—Heather's leaving time— when Ivy arrived home. She hurried into the office, carrying her shopping bags, knowing her friend would want to see everything.

'Hi! You're not going to believe this!' Heather exclaimed, swivelling her chair around from the computer table. 'Jordan has just ordered twenty dozen red roses, without the fudge, to be couriered to a Palm Beach residence on Friday afternoon.' Her brow furrowed over this departure from form. 'What do you suppose this means?'

Ivy grinned at her. 'I guess they're to decorate his mother's house for our engagement party on Saturday night.' She held out her left hand. 'Look!'

Heather squealed and erupted from her chair, pouncing on Ivy's hand, her eyes goggling at the ring. 'Oh, wow! That's the best Christmas tree I've ever seen!'

Ivy laughed. 'It does look a bit like one.'

'And marrying Jordan Powell!' She grinned in delight. 'All your Christmases have come at once, Ivy. Why didn't you call me, tell me? It's such fantastic news!'

'*Fantastic* is the operative word,' Ivy answered dryly. 'It didn't seem real at first. I wasn't expecting it. You know why, Heather.'

'That's all in the past,' was Heather's blithe dismissal. 'I thought he was seriously attracted to you and this proves it. Let's go out to the kitchen, pour ourselves a celebratory drink and you can tell me all the marvellous details.' Her eyes sparkled gleefully. 'Did he go down on bended knee to propose?'

Ivy shook her head. 'It wasn't like that.'

She didn't mind revealing the truth to Heather, who knew all the background. They sat at the kitchen table and Ivy poured out her feelings, how Jordan had turned them around, and confiding that she was still coming to grips with the new situation and would be grateful for any input that might help with it.

'Let Jordan be your guide into his world, Ivy,' Heather advised. 'Trust him to decide what's best for both of you. I think he's been doing that already, and he'll go on doing it because he loves you and doesn't want to lose you. Just keep that straight in your mind and don't let other people mess with it. Not his mother, not his sister, not anyone.'

'Yes, you're right,' Ivy agreed, the load of worries lifting from her heart. She could do this—be Jordan's partner in life. Anything worth having was worth working at. With experience would come more expertise in handling whatever had to be handled for them to be happy together.

'Now about this engagement party. Are Graham and I invited?' Heather asked hopefully.

'Of course! And all our other friends, as well.'

'Oh, good! We can hire a minibus for the night and have the fun of going together.'

There were calls to be made, arrangements to be put in place, and knowing she had the happy support of her friends made the prospect of the engagement party much less intimidating. As for the rest, she would have Jordan at her side—her man, proclaiming to the whole world that she was his woman.

It should be—would be—the most wonderful night of her life!

Jordan left no stone unturned to ensure there would be no upsetting incident for Ivy at their engagement party. The roses were a good talking point. Not only did they identify Ivy as a clever businesswoman, but it would undoubtedly amuse people to hear he'd been ordering them from her farm for years and she had initially rejected him because of them. Laughter was always an effective icebreaker and they would look at Ivy with the respect she deserved.

Having dealt with the business of the day, he drove to Palm Beach, intent on checking what his mother and sister had done so far. It was already Wednesday. Much had to be accomplished in three days, but where there was a will, there was a way, especially when cost was no object. Jordan didn't care what was paid out for this occasion. It had to be right for Ivy.

'I'm exhausted,' his mother complained, the moment the butler had shown him into the lounge room where pre-dinner drinks had been served. 'I've been on the telephone all day, letting people know, begging my favourite caterer to drop everything for me...'

'Which, of course, he did,' Jordan dryly remarked. No one refused Nonie Powell.

She set down her glass of sherry and threw up her hands in exasperation. 'Why the hurry? She's not pregnant, is she?'

'No. I just don't want Ivy in any doubt as to where she stands with me,' he replied, his gaze moving to his sister who was nursing a large Scotch on the rocks. 'Before you dull your sensibilities with alcohol, I'd like you to give me your support in doing that, Olivia.'

'I deserve a drink,' she retorted, her chin lifting belligerently. 'I've been on the phone for you all day, too.'

'Thank you. I hope it wasn't too much of a hardship.' He was quite sure she'd had a ball, getting the gossip-mill going as well as spreading the happy news. 'What I want now is for you to write Ivy a letter, apologising for your behaviour towards her yesterday and expressing the hope you can be friends in the future. If it's posted tomorrow for next-day delivery, she'll receive it before the weekend and feel more comfortable about meeting you again on Saturday night.'

Olivia huffed, grimaced, then lifted eyes full of confusion. 'I honestly thought she was getting into you, Jordan. How was I to know that you loved each other? You've never been serious about a woman. Certainly not since Biancha Barlow almost had you fooled.'

Ivy's character was light years away from Biancha's. 'Ivy doesn't want me for my money,' he said with absolute certainty. 'I've known that for quite a while. This morning I wanted to buy her some jewellery to match the engagement ring. She recoiled from it as though I'd offered her a snake. I think you've poisoned her mind against accepting any expensive gifts from me, Olivia, and I need you to put that right. I want her to be happy about what I can give her, not feel branded as a fortune-hunter.'

Olivia frowned. 'What jewellery did she knock back?'

'A necklace and earrings in emeralds and diamonds to match the ring.'

Her eyes almost popped. 'Wow! That's big!'

Jordan bored in. 'I wanted her to have them, Olivia. If you hadn't interfered...'

'Yes, yes, I see your point. I made it nasty instead of nice.' She set her drink down and rose to her feet with an air of decision. 'I'll go to the office and write the letter now. And Jordan...' She gave him a crooked little smile. 'I'm glad for you. I really am. At least one of us might have a happy marriage.'

He smiled back. 'Thank you.'

It was the first time he'd actually felt a sympathetic bond with his sister. Maybe, if Olivia made the effort to be friends with Ivy, he and she could become closer in the future, set their usual antagonism aside and be warmer towards each other.

Strange how suddenly his whole life now seemed centred on Ivy. Marriage to her had not entered his mind until it had burst into it as the only way to stop her from leaving him. Yet it was beginning to feel more and more right, so much so he was determined to prevent any possible snag that might stop it from happening.

'It's only been three months since Sacha Thornton's exhibition,' his mother commented, viewing him with sceptical eyes. 'You're rushing into this, Jordan.'

He raised challenging eyebrows. 'I was told it was only three weeks after you met Dad that he asked you to marry him.'

She waved a dismissive hand. 'They were different times.'

He shook his head. 'People have the same feelings now as they had then, Mum.'

That earned a hard look. 'You're sure she's right for you?'

'Yes.' Doubts could come later, but Jordan was now bent on not entertaining them until they bit him.

'Different backgrounds,' his mother pointed out.

'Doesn't matter.'

'It will in the future.'

'Not if we don't let it.'

She sighed. 'Well, I see you have your mind set on it, Jordan, but it is a different world now and women won't put up with what they used to. Do you honestly think you'll be faithful to her in a long-term relationship?'

He hadn't put that question to himself yet he answered without the slightest hesitation. 'Yes, I do. I've had lots of women in the past, Mum. I know I've got the best with Ivy. I won't even be tempted to look elsewhere.'

She sighed again. 'Yes, I guess you do know that.' Her eyes had a wry look as she added, 'Your father didn't. I was a virgin when we married and I was never really comfortable with what he wanted in bed. In some ways it was a relief when his mistresses supplied it. I knew he would never leave me, but…it wasn't the happiest of marriages, Jordan. I hope you have a better one with your Ivy.'

Jordan found himself deeply touched by this confession and sad that his mother had never known uninhibited joy in sex. 'I'm sorry it was like that for you, Mum. And for Dad. Do you think it was right for you to stay together all those years?'

Nonie's pride answered him. 'I had a wonderful life with your father. I wouldn't have given it up for anything. Besides, we had our family. And your father wouldn't have given that up for anything.'

Family…no, he wouldn't give that up, either, if he and Ivy had children. He had to make this marriage work, on every level. Sex was no problem. He was sure it never would be. If they could strike the right balance with the living part, if Ivy would ease up over fitting into his scene…

'This party is important to me, Mum,' he confided, appealing for her understanding, as well as her help. 'I want Ivy to believe she can have a wonderful life with me. Please…will you ask your friends to be especially kind to her? Olivia did quite a lot of damage to her confidence. If you give her your approval…'

'Jordan, I don't know the girl. I've barely met her.'

'I'm asking you to do it because it's important to me. I can handle the rest but I *need* this from you. Use your power, your influence, to make it a great night for Ivy. I know you can do it.'

Reluctance flashed in her eyes. 'You're putting my judgement of character on the line. What if she lets you down later?'

'Do it out of respect for *my* judgement.'

She stared at him, will clashing against will. Jordan poured every atom of forceful energy into his stare back. 'I've never let you down, Mum,' he said quietly. 'Anything you've asked of me…'

'All right,' she snapped. 'I'll do it. I just hope she lives up to your judgement, Jordan.'

He smiled.

The groundwork was laid.

All that remained was for Ivy to come to the party.

# CHAPTER SIXTEEN

THE story of Jordan Powell's engagement to a rose farmer was front-page news in Saturday's newspapers. Jordan had warned Ivy he'd been asked for a press release, and she was safely installed at his Balmoral home before details of their romance were publicly released, escaping from the attention of the paparazzi, who subsequently swarmed to the farm to photograph everything in sight, and a bunch of reporters wanting more personal stories about her.

Heather and Graham held the fort, declaring she was a wonderful employer, there was no dirt to dig up and everything in the garden was rosy. Sacha was also approached for comment, to which she had no comment apart from saying her beautiful daughter deserved a beautiful man and she confidently expected them both to have a beautiful marriage.

After the umpteenth call telling her what was happening, Ivy rolled her eyes at Jordan and wailed, 'Please tell me this is a one-day wonder.'

He laughed and drew her into a reassuring embrace. 'It's a one-day wonder. Truly. Just the surprise element sparking it off. There's nothing to get their teeth into. And we'll be in Europe next week. Nothing to follow up with.'

She sighed and nestled closer. 'That's a relief.'

'There will be a society columnist and photographer at the party tonight, but I'll be right at your side and they won't cause you any unpleasantness. They're my mother's pet media people. Okay?'

She looked him in the eye and solemnly promised, 'I'll do my best to get used to being publicly connected to you, Jordan. I'll learn how to handle it.'

'Don't worry about it, Ivy. The trick is not to let it really touch you. We live our lives regardless of what people print or say.'

She smiled as she reached up and touched his face. 'I'll have to grow some armour like you.'

The Ned Kelly paintings in Jordan's bedroom reflected her comment as Ivy dressed for the party. She'd chosen to wear black, like the armour of the famous bushranger. Black was safe. No one was going to criticise an elegant black dress, and it *was* elegant. The bodice fell from a beaded yoke to a beaded waistband, leaving her shoulders and arms bare. The crepe fabric was cut on the bias for the long skirt so it clung to her hips, then dropped in graceful folds to her feet. She did not have to wear killer shoes with it, which was also safe. And pain-free. It was important to her to feel comfortable tonight. In every sense.

The style of the dress didn't need a necklace. The long jet earrings she'd bought for the sequinned outfit looked right with it. The diamond and emerald earrings Jordan had wanted to buy her would have looked spectacular, but to her mind, they would have distracted people—perhaps unkindly—from the ring, which was spectacular enough on its own.

A last check of her appearance assured Ivy she was suitably armoured for the role of Jordan Powell's fiancée.

Black was the best foil for her pale skin and the riot of wavy red hair fluffed out around her bare shoulders. In fact, she couldn't remember ever looking better than she did right now.

Having fastened a small black beaded evening bag containing repair make-up around her wrist, she headed downstairs to parade for Margaret who wanted to see her in her finery. Jordan's housekeeper had seen him in a formal black dinner suit many times, but Ivy had always worn casual clothes at Balmoral. Tonight was different in so many ways, Ivy's heart started skittering nervously as she saw both Margaret and Jordan waiting for her at the foot of the staircase.

They both looked up. Ivy held her shoulders straight and descended with as much aplomb as she could muster, determined to look as though she was born to be at Jordan's side. Margaret clapped her hands at the performance, grinning from ear to ear in delight.

'Will I do?' Ivy asked, wanting to hear their approval in words.

'You'll do perfectly!' Margaret answered emphatically.

'Perfectly!' Jordan echoed, the blaze of desire in his eyes flooding her with warmth.

She wanted him, too. Which was what all this was about…wanting each other for the rest of their lives. It was easy to keep that in the forefront of her mind as they travelled to Palm Beach. Ray drove them in the Bentley, and sitting beside Jordan in the back seat, his fingers tightly interlaced with hers reinforcing the strong sexual connection between them, Ivy began to feel confident that nothing would separate them.

She had never been to his mother's home. Jordan's house was big and impressive but nowhere near on the same scale as the Mediterranean-style mansion at Palm Beach, with its three storeys of columns and balconies. It screamed opulent wealth, making Ivy super-conscious of stepping into a different world. But she had Jordan as her guide. And partner. She didn't have to be dreadfully nervous about it.

Security guards flanked the entrance gateway, ensuring that only invited guests passed by them. Jordan had planned to be the last to arrive, preferring an informal meet-and-greet as they moved around the party, which was now obviously in full swing. As they alighted from the Bentley, dance music and a distant babble of voices could be heard. Ivy hoped her friends were enjoying themselves.

A butler met them at the front door. They stepped into a grand foyer where a magnificent display of her red roses stood on a marble pedestal. It put a smile on Ivy's face, her eyes twinkling at Jordan, who she knew had organised that, too. The butler ushered them into an incredibly fabulous ballroom: massive crystal chandeliers, mirrored walls, gorgeous sofas, chairs and ornamental tables ringing the dance floor, and doors opening out to a balcony at the end of it.

A live band was playing from a dais in one of the far corners. Most of the younger guests were kicking up their heels on the dance floor. Ivy spotted Heather and Graham amongst them. The rest of the crowd were sitting or standing around chatting, helping themselves to whatever was being offered on the trays of food and drinks being circulated by an army of waiters.

Nonie Powell rose from a chaise longue and came forward to greet them, her royal-blue satin evening dress adding to her queenly air. Sacha detached herself from a group of people, trailing eagerly after her, very much the colourful butterfly in a bright orange silk pantsuit with a long split jacket in shades of violet, blue and turquoise and printed with orange and red flowers. She wasn't actually wearing bells but lots of gold necklaces and bangles were jingling.

The contrast between the mothers was huge.

Totally different backgrounds, Ivy thought, hoping it would never become a divisive issue. Congratulatory kisses were bestowed. Jordan's mother drew them over to a seated group of her closest friends to introduce Ivy. They were all very gracious to her, amused that Jordan had finally been *caught,* saying Ivy must have many admirable qualities to make him drop his playboy mantle, and wanting to hear their plans for the future. The conversation was easy, fun, and Ivy began to relax and enjoy herself.

After they'd posed for the society photographer for a few happy snaps, Olivia dragged them away, declaring her friends were insisting on an audience with the newly engaged couple. Ivy instantly seized the opportunity to thank Jordan's sister for her letter, saying she hoped they could be friends in the future, too.

'Just don't bring any poison into my brother's life and you'll have my respect forever,' Olivia replied, bubbling over with high spirits.

Champagne was flowing and all the introductions were carried out with good humour. Jordan fed it with his charm, satisfying the curiosity about their relationship with amusing stories of how hard he'd had to work to win her. The women admired the ring. The men admired her as a woman. Ivy felt herself being scrutinised from head to foot by both genders but there was no real discomfort from it. The general flow of approval put her at ease.

'The pair of you look fantastic together,' Heather whispered to her in passing. 'You're slaying 'em, Ivy. No worries.'

The only worry was in trying to remember the names of so many people. Jordan helped by repeating them throughout the conversations. On the whole, Ivy thought she was coping fairly well, but she was glad when Jordan insisted they be excused because he couldn't wait any longer to dance with her.

It was a relief to be alone together for a little while, to simply sink into Jordan's embrace and feel at one with him. The slow beat of the jazz waltz thumped through her heart, giving her a dreamy sense of contentment. This was her man and he was the best partner she could ever have to spend her life with.

'Happy?' he murmured, dropping a hot kiss on her hair.

She lifted her head up from his shoulder to shoot him a brilliant smile. 'Very happy.'

He smiled back, the sexy simmer in his eyes giving her a buzz of pleasure. Making love tonight was going to be extra special. She wished they could leave now, but…

'Please excuse me, Mr Powell. I have a message for Miss Thornton.'

It was the butler, startling them both with his intrusion on the dance floor. What message couldn't wait a few more minutes until the music ended?

'Some problem, Lloyd?' Jordan asked, frowning at him.

'Mrs Powell sent me to tell Miss Thornton her father has arrived.'

'My father?' Ivy cried in astonishment. 'There must be some mistake. My father died over two years ago.'

The butler shook his head in dismayed confusion. 'I have no knowledge of this. The man was not on the guest list but he showed identification and explained that he'd been in Melbourne on business and didn't think he could make it to the party on such short notice. However, he'd managed to get an evening flight and didn't want to miss such a special occasion for his daughter. It seemed reasonable...'

'He's an imposter,' Ivy insisted, appalled that anyone would try such an offensive stunt.

'We'll very quickly sort it out,' Jordan assured her. 'Thank you, Lloyd. Not your fault you weren't aware of Ivy's family situation. Though my mother should have been. I told her.'

His frown deepened as he steered Ivy off the dance floor. 'Let's find Sacha first,' he muttered. 'Confront the guy with both of you.'

'Yes,' she agreed, her stomach churning at having to face the disgusting con-man. She wanted her mother there for back-up.

They found her out on the balcony with a group of her friends. Ivy quickly collected her for a private discussion with Jordan. As they joined him she was anxiously explaining, 'A man has come here claiming to be my father, presenting some identification that has to be false. I need you to...'

Sacha stopped dead, shock draining the colour from her face. 'No! No!' The fierce denials exploded off her tongue. Her eyes glazed over.

Ivy grabbed her around the waist to support her, worrying that she was going to faint. It was awful, someone stepping into a dead man's shoes to make some sensational situation, especially when her real father had been dearly loved. 'I'm sorry,' she blurted out. 'It was a shock to me, too. He's with Jordan's mother, and we have to denounce him, Sacha, before he makes more mischief.'

A shudder ran through Sacha. The limpness was shaken off by a surge of outrage. 'How dare he!' She looked at Ivy with wildly ferocious eyes. 'How dare he after all these years! The rotten snake in the grass!'

'Who?' Ivy asked, feeling a flutter of fear.

Sacha turned to Jordan in fighting determination. 'We have to get rid of him. For Ivy's sake. Order your security people to take him away and keep him away.'

'But who is it?' Ivy pleaded, not understanding anything.

'Your father's brother! Dick Thornton! Tricky Dicky!' It was a snarl of hatred. 'I haven't seen him since before you were born, Ivy, but I know him to be a total bastard without any conscience whatsoever. You can bet he's come to try and make some capital out of your connection to Jordan. It's the kind of lousy thing he'd do.'

An uncle! Her father had never mentioned having a brother. His parents—her grandparents—had died before she was born, and he'd told her they were on their own, just the two of them, plus Sacha when they had weekends together.

'Right! Let's go and undo the mischief he's already made,' Jordan said grittily, his handsome face instantly settling into a look of formidable power.

He hooked his arm around Ivy's to carry her along with him. She felt too dazed by the idea of having a wicked uncle to even begin to comprehend what it might mean to her. Sacha marched ahead of them, the panels of her split jacket flying out with the furious energy driving her forward.

The man standing beside Nonie Powell near the entrance to the ballroom had the gall to smile at their approach, not the least bit alarmed at the prospect of being unmasked as an imposter. He cut quite a fine figure in his formal black suit. He'd certainly made himself presentable. There were still some threads of ginger in his greying hair. The straight line of his nose was very similar to her father's, as was the distinctive slant of his eyebrows. Ivy sucked in a sharp breath as his eyes—green eyes—targeted her with dancing delight.

It was easy to understand why Nonie Powell had not denied him entry to the party. The family resemblance, the name of Thornton, would have given her pause for further investigation. However, she had discreetly held him aside from the known guests, waiting for confirmation of his claim, for which Ivy was intensely grateful.

'Well, well, I didn't know what a beautiful daughter I had,' the man rolled out as they arrived to deal with him.

'She's not yours! She was never yours!' her mother declared in towering outrage.

'Still as exotic as ever, Sacha,' he tossed at her, his smile broadening, not dimming at her rebuttal of his claim. 'You make me remember now why I couldn't resist you.'

'Don't think you'll get away with anything this time,' she fired back at him. 'Robert's gone so I don't have his feelings to consider.'

'Poor Robert, who was left sterile from his stint in Vietnam,' he drawled mockingly. 'You must have had to 'fess up to him that it was me who got you pregnant. And you know and I know that DNA will prove it. So let's cut to the chase, shall we? Our lucky daughter has hit the jackpot and I'm here to collect my share of it or the skeletons will come out of the closet with a vengeance.' He smiled at Jordan. 'I can't imagine the high and mighty Powell family would like that.'

'Jordan?' his mother bit out in tight disapproval. 'I did bring up background to you.'

'We all have skeletons in the closet, don't we, Mum?' he answered blandly. 'Let's take this to the library for a more in-depth discussion out of the public eye.'

'Yes,' she snapped, turning haughtily to escape the threat of embarrassing scandal. 'If you'll accompany me, Mr Thornton?'

'With pleasure, Mrs Powell.'

All five of them left the ballroom in Nonie Powell's wake.

Ivy's mind was reeling over the revelations of the last few minutes. Her whole being recoiled from accepting this man as her biological father. Was it true? Did his story have some substance? He'd seemed totally confident that a DNA test would prove his claim of paternity.

Sacha had called him a rotten snake in the grass and clearly that was what he was.

Poison.

And she had unwittingly brought him into Jordan's life.

Poison Ivy.

Her heart sank.

If she was the illegitimate daughter of a blackmailer, how would Jordan feel about this? Would he still want her at his side? He hated blackmail and dealt ruthlessly with it. Maybe he would see separating himself from her as the only way to stop the flow of more and more poison.

# CHAPTER SEVENTEEN

THE library was another enormous room; its walls lined with books, a collection of decorative globes of the world adding interest, a huge mahogany desk at one end, two black leather chesterfields facing each other across a parquet coffee table, several black leather armchairs grouped in front of the desk as though ready for a conference.

Jordan led Ivy to one of these and saw her seated, murmuring, 'Don't worry. I'll take care of this.'

She lifted anguished eyes. 'I didn't know anything about this man.'

'We must get to the truth now, Ivy. Bear with it,' he advised her, relentless purpose stamped on his face.

She cringed inside, frightened of what else was to be revealed. As Jordan insisted they all be seated and rounded the desk to take the chair behind it, she stared at her mother who had kept this background hidden from her all her life. Sacha was glaring at Dick Thornton with utter loathing. Her blood-red nails were digging into the leather armrest as though wanting to claw him to death.

He sat at perfect ease, his legs casually crossed, a smug little smile lingering on his mouth. Nonie Powell ignored both of them, sitting straight-backed and stiff-faced as she watched her son take what must have been his father's chair and adopt the air of a formidable chairman who was not about to tolerate any nonsense from anyone at this gathering.

'Sacha, Ivy believes that her father is dead,' he started, boring straight to the vital point. 'Is that true or not?'

'Robert *was* her father,' she insisted vehemently. 'Ivy could not have had a better one. From the day she was born, he loved her and wanted to take care of her. And he did. No father could have been more devoted to his daughter.' She shot a pleading look at Ivy. 'You know that's true.'

'Yes,' Ivy agreed, the word coming out huskily as a lump of grief lodged in her throat.

'Was he her biological father?' Jordan asked.

Sacha sucked in a deep breath and shot another look of loathing at the man seated beside her. 'No, he wasn't. This disgusting rat raped me when I thwarted his plan to talk his brother out of his inheritance. I was left pregnant, and when I couldn't hide it from Robert any more, he insisted on marrying me and bringing up the child as his.'

'Hey, hey, hey!' Dick Thornton protested. 'You didn't yell rape at the time, Sacha. There was a lot of free love going on in that house, as you well know.'

'Free love?' Nonie Powell queried waspishly.

'Only between consenting adults,' Sacha shot at her before turning back to the bad brother in bitter accusation. 'You knew why I didn't call the police. None of us could afford to go anywhere else. We were barely scraping along on part-time jobs in between attending college or uni and studying for our courses. I couldn't risk having us all evicted.'

'Why would you be evicted?' Jordan asked.

Dick Thornton gave a bark of derisive laughter. 'Because they were squatters. A whole bunch of hippie squatters living it up in a deserted mansion.'

'We weren't doing any harm,' Sacha fiercely declared.

'Squatters,' Nonie Powell said in a tone of horror.

Sacha rounded on her. 'Most of us were poor students without any family money to support us. And before you turn your nose up at us, let me tell you, one of them is now the top medical expert in the world in his field. Another is a highly regarded barrister. Yet another went on to become a famous film-maker. I can name names if you feel it necessary to check up on them.'

She turned her gaze anxiously to Ivy. 'Robert was adrift when he came back from Vietnam. No one wanted to know about what our soldiers suffered there. No one wanted to help them. We should never have been in that war in the first place. Robert was a conscripted soldier, sent to do his duty by his country, then treated like dirt to be swept under the mat when he returned. He found refuge in that house of free-spirited students. He tended the garden and grew vegetables for us. He wanted to nurture life, not destroy it, and we were happy there…'

Tears glittered in her eyes. She dashed them away to glare her hatred at Dick Thornton again. 'Until his brother came, preying on Robert's sense of family, saying he didn't need his part of their inheritance to build a future because he was sterile and had no future.'

'If you'd kept your big mouth shut, Sacha, Robert would have turned what our parents left him over to me and you'd have gone on your own merry way, just smelling the roses,' he said mockingly.

Sheer rage erupted. 'You sick bastard! You set out to make Robert feel worthless and he wasn't. He had the right to build a life for himself and I wasn't going to let you take the money he could buy a farm with.'

'So you stuck your oar in and I stuck mine in,' he retorted in a crass jeer.

'By raping her as payback for interfering,' Jordan inserted quietly.

'Gave me a lot of satisfaction,' Dick Thornton admitted with relish, then quickly checked himself. 'Her word against mine in any court of law. Besides, it's all water under the bridge. What counts now is you wanting to marry my beautiful daughter and me wanting a slice of her good fortune.'

'Jordan, you cannot submit to a blackmailer,' Nonie Powell stated in high dudgeon. 'This marriage is clearly unsuitable. Best that you walk away from it right now.'

'Ivy is totally innocent of any wrongdoing!' Sacha snapped at her. 'Can you say the same of your own daughter, Nonie?'

Although it had to be a blind hit, it caused Nonie Powell to press her lips together. She looked at Ivy in angry reproof, as though Sacha had learned of Olivia's problems from her. Which wasn't true. She hadn't spoken a word to anyone about Ashton's attempt at blackmail.

Jordan flicked a querying look at her.

She shook her head, but the implication that she might have blabbed sickened her. No relationship could work without trust. As it was, she wasn't sure their relationship could survive tonight's revelations.

Her mind was awash with the flood of information about both her parents and the situation which had brought them together and led to their marriage—a marriage of need and compassion and love which she hadn't understood until now. Robert and Sacha were good people but that didn't matter, any more than her own innocence of any wrong-doing mattered. There was no escaping the fact that she was the daughter of a rapist, and would be forever tainted by this rotten man.

Jordan sat in silence, weighing up what he'd heard so far. He had instinctively dismissed his mother's solution—*walk away from it*—though that would, of course, extract him from this nasty mess. If it was only lust driving him to keep Ivy in his life…if he still actually anticipated a marriage that only lasted as long as their passion ran hot…why bother dealing with this scum?

He looked at Ivy.

She shook her head as though she'd already given up on the idea of a future together, her eyes sick and despairing, her face totally stricken by all she'd been hearing.

His heart went out to her.

He knew in that instant that this woman meant more to him than anything else in his life. No doubts. No doubts about their future together, either. Nothing on earth could make him walk away from her. He had to fight the urge to get up and take her out of all this right now. The situation had to be resolved first or she'd be haunted by it. He would not let it come between them. Ever.

He turned a stern gaze to his mother. 'In our family, there have been private matters which we've preferred not to bare, Mum. Let's not make hasty judgements on others. I see no fault in Sacha. And certainly not in Ivy. I'd appreciate it if you'd refrain from any further reactive comment and take into account the nobility of decisions made for the good of others. That deserves respect and admiration, not criticism.'

Nonie frowned at him, not used to being chastised for her behaviour and affronted that it be done in front of others, but she hadn't given any consideration to Ivy's feelings and it was well past time she started giving some consideration to how he felt, too.

'While we're on the subject of noble sacrifices, let's get to how much you'll sacrifice for my silence,' Dick Thornton said cheerfully. 'Make it good and you can all play happy families again.'

Jordan wiped everything else from his mind and concentrated on drawing out what was needed. 'How much do you think your silence is worth?' he asked coldly.

'Well, I'm sure parts of the media would gobble up a story like this. Hippie headquarters in a deserted mansion, free love amongst the squatters, brother pitted against brother by our gorgeous butterfly artist, the baby she dumped on one brother to be free to pursue her own career....'

'I did not dump Ivy!' Sacha cried, unable to contain her fury at the malignment. 'She was happy with Robert.' Her gaze turned pleadingly to her daughter. 'I tried living on the farm. I helped Robert start it and worked along with him, but it wasn't the kind of life I wanted and Robert knew it. The artist in me craved much more of the world but he had seen too much of it in Vietnam and the farm was the only world he wanted. He insisted that I go, said I'd given him his life and he wanted to give me mine. We still had weekends together, at the farm or in the city. I didn't dump you, Ivy. I simply couldn't take you away from Robert. You were so much *his* little girl.'

'Except she wasn't,' Thornton mocked. 'And that

lie makes *my* story all the more credible and valuable, doesn't it, Mr Powell? Lovely fruity fodder for gossip.'

Jordan held up a warning hand to Sacha, not wanting her to interrupt again. 'Name your price, Mr Thornton.'

'Oh, I won't be too greedy,' Dick Thornton drawled, believing he was in the box seat. 'Given the fact that you're a billionaire, I think five million dollars is a relatively modest amount.'

'You want five million dollars from me or you'll make your version of the past public. Is that what you're threatening?' Jordan bored in.

'In a nutshell, yes,' Thornton replied, grinning from ear to ear.

'Thank you.'

'No!' Ivy leapt up from her chair, anguished eyes begging him to understand. 'You mustn't do it, Jordan. This will only be the start.' She tugged at the ring he'd put on her finger as she headed for the desk. 'Whatever he says won't be worth anything if I don't marry you. Take this ring back.' She laid it on the desk. 'You can say it was a mistake ever to get involved with me.' Tears pooled in her eyes. 'It was. I always knew it was…just a fantasy.'

'That's not true,' Jordan answered her firmly, picking up the ring and rising to his feet. 'It was right! It was always *right,* Ivy. And I'm not about to let you down.'

'But…' Her hands fluttered in despair as the tears trickled down her cheeks.

Jordan caught her hands and slid the ring back on her finger, his eyes burning through her tears with an intensity of purpose that could not be broken. 'We're going to be together for the rest of our lives.'

And if it hadn't been clear to his mother before

why he loved this woman and wanted her as his wife, it should be crystal-clear now, as she witnessed Ivy's anguish over this situation and her willingness to free him from it.

'Bravo!' Thornton crowed, clapping his hands at what he believed was his triumph.

Jordan shot him a sharply derisive look. 'Bravo, indeed, Mr Thornton. You could not have done a better job of incriminating yourself.'

'So what?' Thornton retorted, totally unruffled. 'It's in everyone's interests here to keep this private.'

Jordan hugged Ivy's shoulders, tucking her close to him, wanting her to feel both comforted and protected as he confronted the slime who so richly deserved some comeuppance.

'My father occasionally held business meetings in this library. He installed a mechanism in his desk to record them. I switched it on when I sat down. Should you go to any section of the media to sell your story, the first action they will take will be to check with me. I will then take the tape to the police and proceed with criminal charges.'

'The story will still get out,' Thornton countered belligerently.

'No one will buy it, and you, sir, will go to jail without any money.'

'Oh, bravo!' It was Sacha this time, clapping her hands with sweet relief at some justice finally being done to the man who had tried to swindle his brother and raped her because she'd frustrated his scheme.

Jordan directed a commanding look at his mother. 'Time to call in a couple of your security men, Mum. Best that our uninvited visitor be discreetly escorted from the premises.'

Nonie was up from her chair and sweeping out of the library before Dick Thornton had fully processed the fact that his scheme was defeated and *he* was about to be evicted.

'Now look here!' he blustered, rising from his chair to fight his corner. 'I can still cause you embarrassment, turning up at your society events and telling all and sundry I'm Ivy's dad. It must be worth something to you to have me stay away. That's not blackmail. You can't have me jailed for that.'

'I can have you arrested for harassment,' Jordan answered, not the least bit concerned by his threat. 'I doubt a dad who deserted his daughter before she was born will be seen as having any rights at all. Why invite trouble when there'll be no profit in it for you?'

That salient point gave the slimy con-man a momentary pause for thought. He then shot a vicious look at Ivy. 'What about her? I can get to her when you're not around. Buy me off and you can live in peace.'

Feeling Ivy shiver, Jordan hugged her more tightly and spoke with totally ruthless determination. 'Do you want to be put under surveillance for the rest of your life, every dodgy move you make watched and reported on? As you pointed out, I'm a billionaire and I will go to any lengths—regardless of cost—to protect the woman I'm going to marry. I'll pay whatever price I have to in order to preserve her peace, but not to you, Dick Thornton. I will never pay you a cent, and I'll make you pay if you ever give Ivy any further distress. You can count on that.'

The extent of Jordan's power and the relentless threat of it finally penetrated. The man stared back at him, the fight draining out of his face. He threw up his hands in defeat as Nonie Powell led two security guards into the library.

'Okay. Call your dogs off,' he snarled. 'I won't bother you again.'

'Oh, I think I'll have them stay on your tail, at least until you move to another city and make a life for yourself away from all of us,' Jordan said to reinforce what he was prepared to do to ensure freedom from this man's poison. Having cast the con-man a look of towering contempt, he addressed the guards. 'Take this man to wherever he is currently housed and arrange to have him kept under constant surveillance until further notice.'

'I told you I won't bother you again,' Thornton cried in panicky protest.

'No, you won't. I'll see that you don't,' Jordan promised him. 'I'd advise you to go quietly now. The idea of putting you on trial and sending you to jail is becoming more compelling by the moment. In fact...'

'I'm going! I'm going!'

He went, closely escorted by the two security guards. Jordan was confident that Thornton would drop out of their lives as abruptly as he'd come into them. Nevertheless, he would keep a check on the con-man's movements, just for extra assurance.

As soon as the door closed behind them he turned to his mother. 'Mum, you and Sacha should return to the party now, preferably arm in arm, presenting a united front. I suggest you indicate you've had a happy chat about the forthcoming wedding. Any questions about Dick Thornton you dismiss by saying he was simply a brash party-crasher pretending to be someone he wasn't. Which is true. Robert Thornton was Ivy's father.'

'Yes, he was,' Sacha agreed with feeling, turning an apologetic face to Nonie. 'I'm sorry this was all such a shock, Nonie, but the past is the past and I've put it behind me for so many years, I never imagined it would...'

'We'll move on,' his mother cut in with her lofty air. 'We must do as Jordan says to save any unpleasant tattle.'

His mother was well-practised at sweeping unpleasantness under the mat and keeping it there. He had no doubt she would handle the situation with her usual queenly aplomb and guide Ivy's mother into following her lead.

'Yes. Yes, of course,' Sacha agreed distractedly. She threw an anxious look back at Ivy as they moved towards the door. 'Robert and I...we never meant you to know how you came to be born. I'm so sorry you've heard about it like this, but it doesn't really matter, Ivy. You've always been loved. Very much.'

Ivy nodded. She couldn't speak. Tears had welled into her eyes again and emotional turmoil was still churning through her. The horror of Dick Thornton, the circumstances of her birth, the background of her parents' marriage, her upbringing on the farm, Jordan's determination to rid her of the nightmare of her biological father and fix every problem that could mar their life together...her mind was jammed with so many feelings it was impossible to think of what she should say or how to say it.

The two mothers made their exit together.

Jordan turned her towards him. 'And you're loved even more now,' he said in his richly charming voice, the bedroom-blue eyes promising her it was true as he gently stroked the wetness from her cheeks. 'I love you, Ivy, and come what may in our lives, I'll never let you down.'

The sickening sense that what she had believed about her life had shifted into something else, and was still shifting as she gained a clearer understanding of how everything had come about, lost its grip on her. Jordan was making the present and what they shared in it far more important.

Faced with a situation that could have shattered everything between them, he had not let her down.

She believed he never would. He was a rock of solid support. She could trust him to be always there for her, no matter what.

Their relationship wasn't a mistake.

It wasn't a fantasy that would come crashing down to earth.

Her heart trembled at the amazing commitment Jordan was giving her. Had given her throughout this terrible showdown with Dick Thornton. Had been giving her all along, from his patient waiting in the coffee shop. She lifted a hand to stroke his cheek in awe of his masterful determination to make what felt right…really right.

'I love you, too,' she said huskily. 'Thank you for…for standing by me. I'll always stand by you in the future. I promise you that, Jordan.'

He smiled teasingly. 'No more giving me up to save me from trouble.'

'No.' She managed a shaky smile back. 'Wild horses won't tear me away.'

'Good!'

A lingering niggle of anxiety remained in her mind. 'I didn't tell Sacha about Olivia's blackmail problem. Please trust me on that, Jordan. I wouldn't gossip about anything so private and hurtful. Your mother obviously thought I had, and you looked at me as though you wondered.'

He shook his head. 'Not because I was wondering about that, Ivy. I was thinking how very wrong about you my mother was, and how very much you suited me, in every sense.'

'Oh! ' It was wonderful to have the trust issue so summarily dismissed. Jordan believed her as absolutely as she believed him.

'And don't be worrying about our respective mothers coming to open blows about their differences,' he went on, speaking very dryly as he added, 'I'm sure they're both strong-minded enough to put them aside as it suits them. They'll think about the future and they'll want to be part of our lives when the grandchildren come along.'

She laughed in sweet relief, realising how well he'd read their mothers' characters. 'How many children would you like to have?'

'As many as you want, my love.' He grinned and added, 'I'm certain to have immense pleasure in making them with you.'

Keeping the rose farm on didn't seem important any more. She would, though, at least through Heather and Graham, but becoming a mother, sharing parenthood with Jordan…that was the future she most wanted…a world of their own making.

'Now let's go and dance,' he said. 'Show the whole world we are one, you and I. Because we are, Ivy. You're my woman and I'm your man and we're going to celebrate our union in front of everyone. That's what this party is about and we're not going to let anyone spoil it.'

'No, we're not,' she agreed, winding her arms around

his neck, her tears completely dried up by the warmth of his pleasure in her, the warmth of his love so manifestly shown to her tonight. 'But kiss me first, Jordan.'

He did.

If eyes followed them to the dance floor, Ivy was totally unaware of them. She was blind to anything but her love for the man who was partnering her...her *life* partner, whose world was her world, just as her world was his. They fitted together. And nothing—nothing whatsoever—was ever going to part them.

## Coming Next Month

from **Harlequin Presents® EXTRA.** Available March 8, 2011.

**#141 A SPANISH BIRTHRIGHT**
**Cathy Williams**
*Wedlocked!*

**#142 UNTOUCHED UNTIL MARRIAGE**
**Chantelle Shaw**
*Wedlocked!*

**#143 HER SINGAPORE FLING**
**Kelly Hunter**
*The Ex Factor*

**#144 GIRLS' GUIDE TO FLIRTING WITH DANGER**
**Kimberly Lang**
*The Ex Factor*

---

# Coming Next Month

from **Harlequin Presents®.** Available March 29, 2011.

**#2981 FLORA'S DEFIANCE**
**Lynne Graham**
*Secretly Pregnant...Conveniently Wed!*

**#2982 THE RETURN OF THE RENEGADE**
**Carole Mortimer**
*The Scandalous St. Claires*

**#2983 NOT FOR SALE**
**Sandra Marton**

**#2984 BEAUTY AND THE GREEK**
**Kim Lawrence**

**#2985 AN ACCIDENTAL BIRTHRIGHT**
**Maisey Yates**

**#2986 THE DEVIL'S HEART**
**Lynn Raye Harris**

# REQUEST YOUR FREE BOOKS!

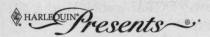 HARLEQUIN *Presents*®

## 2 FREE NOVELS PLUS
## 2 FREE GIFTS!

**YES!** Please send me 2 FREE Harlequin Presents® novels and my 2 FREE gifts (gifts are worth about $10). After receiving them, if I don't wish to receive any more books, I can return the shipping statement marked "cancel." If I don't cancel, I will receive 6 brand-new novels every month and be billed just $4.05 per book in the U.S. or $4.74 per book in Canada. That's a saving of at least 15% off the cover price! It's quite a bargain! Shipping and handling is just 50¢ per book.* I understand that accepting the 2 free books and gifts places me under no obligation to buy anything. I can always return a shipment and cancel at any time. Even if I never buy another book, the two free books and gifts are mine to keep forever.

106/306 HDN E5M4

| | | |
|---|---|---|
| Name | (PLEASE PRINT) | |
| Address | | Apt. # |
| City | State/Prov. | Zip/Postal Code |

Signature (if under 18, a parent or guardian must sign)

### Mail to the **Harlequin Reader Service:**
**IN U.S.A.:** P.O. Box 1867, Buffalo, NY 14240-1867
**IN CANADA:** P.O. Box 609, Fort Erie, Ontario L2A 5X3

Not valid for current subscribers to Harlequin Presents books.

**Are you a current subscriber to Harlequin Presents books and want to receive the larger-print edition? Call 1-800-873-8635 today!**

* Terms and prices subject to change without notice. Prices do not include applicable taxes. N.Y. residents add applicable sales tax. Canadian residents will be charged applicable provincial taxes and GST. Offer not valid in Quebec. This offer is limited to one order per household. All orders subject to approval. Credit or debit balances in a customer's account(s) may be offset by any other outstanding balance owed by or to the customer. Please allow 4 to 6 weeks for delivery. Offer available while quantities last.

**Your Privacy:** Harlequin Books is committed to protecting your privacy. Our Privacy Policy is available online at www.eHarlequin.com or upon request from the Reader Service. From time to time we make our lists of customers available to reputable third parties who may have a product or service of interest to you. If you would prefer we not share your name and address, please check here. ☐

**Help us get it right**—We strive for accurate, respectful and relevant communications. To clarify or modify your communication preferences, visit us at www.ReaderService.com/consumerschoice.

HP10R

*Selene wanted nothing to do with the father of her son, Alex; but Aristedes had other plans...that included them.*

*Read on for an sneak peek from*
*THE SARANTOS SECRET BABY by Olivia Gates,*
*available April 2011, only from Harlequin Desire.*

"You were right to turn my marriage offer down," Aristedes said.

And Selene found her voice at last, found the words that would not betray the blow he'd dealt her. "Thanks for letting me know. You didn't have to come all the way here, though. You could have just let it go. I left yesterday with the understanding that this case is closed."

Before the hot needles behind her eyes could dissolve into an unforgivable display of stupidity and weakness, she began to close the door.

The door stopped against an immovable object. His flat palm.

"I can't accept that." His voice was low, leashed.

What did her tormentor mean now? Was he ending one game only to start another?

She raised eyes as bruised as her self-respect to his, found nothing there but solemnity and determination.

Before she could voice her confusion, he elaborated. "I never let anything go unless I'm certain it's unworkable. I realize I made you an unworkable offer, and that's why I'm withdrawing it. I'm here to offer something else. A workability study."

She leaned against the door, thankful for its support and partial shield. "Your son and I are not a business venture you can test for feasibility."

His gaze grew deeper, made her feel as if he was trying to delve into her mind, take control of it. "It's actually the other way around. I'm the one who would be tested."

She shook her head. "Why bother? I know—and *you* know—you're not workable. Not with me."

His spectacular eyebrows lowered over eyes she felt were emitting silver hypnosis. "You're right again. Neither you nor I have any reason to believe that isn't the truth. The only truth. It might be best for both you and Alex to never hear from me again, to forget I exist. But then again, maybe not. I'm only asking for the chance for both of us to find out for certain. You believe I'm unworkable in any personal relationship. I've lived my life based on that belief about myself. I never really had reason to question it. But I have one now. In fact, I have two."

*Find out what happens in*
*THE SARANTOS SECRET BABY by Olivia Gates,*
*available April 2011, only from Harlequin Desire.*

**Harlequin® Blaze™**

red-hot reads

## Sunny, sensual Hawaiian spring break…again!

Three best girlfriends are recapturing an amazing spring-break vacation they had a decade ago.

First on the beach is former attorney and all-around good girl Mia Butterfield. Meeting up with her boyfriend of old is a bust, so she's shocked when her hero turns out to be someone she'd never have expected…

---

Find out who it is in

# SECOND TIME LUCKY

by acclaimed author

# Debbi Rawlins

---

**Available from Harlequin Blaze® April 2011**

Part of the sensual miniseries,
### *Spring Break*

Part 2: Delicious Do-Over (May)

**Harlequin®**

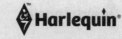 A *Romance* FOR EVERY MOOD™

www.eHarlequin.com

HB79607

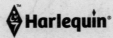

# HARLEQUIN® HISTORICAL:
## Where love is timeless

*USA TODAY*
BESTSELLING AUTHOR
# MARGARET MOORE
INTRODUCES
## *Highland Heiress*

---

## SUED FOR BREACH OF PROMISE!

No sooner does Lady Moira MacMurdaugh breathe a sigh
of relief for avoiding a disastrous marriage to Dunbrachie's
answer to Casanova than she is served with a lawsuit! By
the very man who saved her from a vicious dog attack, no
less: solicitor Gordon McHeath. Torn between loyalty for a
friend and this beautiful woman who stirs him to ridiculous
distraction, Gordon knows he can't have it both ways....

But when sinister forces threaten to upend Lady Moira's world,
Gordon simply can't stand idly by and watch her fall!

**Available from Harlequin Historical**
**April 2011**

### ◆ **Harlequin**®

A *Romance* FOR EVERY MOOD™

www.eHarlequin.com

HH29638